I0590492

Book Cover Design: Meredith Newcom

For Dianne.

I hope you are proud.

Squeeze the Day
by Emelle Gill

1 Mallory

This wasn't the first time I cried in my boss's office. And I ugly cried. Both times.

"Please sit down, Mallory," she said in her soothing spa voice—the kind that makes you want a cucumber water and a deep tissue massage, which felt cruel, considering what came next.

"Our department is downsizing."

That was the official story. Downsizing. Or, if it made the management feel kinder, the company would lay off employees.

My boss is genuinely kind. She didn't want this to happen. She held my hand while I cried, which somehow made it worse. I don't cry often, but something about her calm, nurturing energy turns me into a toddler who's dropped an ice cream cone. The first time I'd cried in her office was over my ex. So she knew what was coming. She prepared for this. I did not.

"I realize this is coming as a shock," she said gently, sliding an open folder across the desk.

Exit paperwork. I see my name on the cover. Very official. Very final.

I snorted. Through tears. Mortifying.

If I'd been paying attention earlier, I might have seen this coming. Fewer people in classes. A quieter spa. Coworkers vanished, as though the steam room had swallowed them whole. It all made business sense.

Unfortunately, business sense doesn't double as a mortgage payment.

Still, I've lived on ramen and cheap frozen burritos before. I can do it again. My situation is not rock bottom—just a plot twist. And apparently, the universe has a weird sense of timing.

The crazy part is, I wanted to do something different and had been dreaming about it for a while, but I told myself every day, "Mallory, don't quit your job. You can't quit until you have something else in place." But I didn't have a Plan B. My backup plan was nonexistent. I also didn't plan on being single at 30. Even this morning, when I got up, I stumbled to the kitchen as usual. I made my coffee, took a shower, and squeezed into my leggings, like every other day. I bundled my hair into a messy bun and put on a layer of sunblock–business as usual.

I thought, "What if I did something different? Something totally out of the box," then went to work, anyway. And now, here we are. So, what the fuck do I do? Get a dog? Move? I guess the world is my oyster; I wish someone would give me a slice of lemon.

I'd worked in gyms and been a personal trainer for ten years. I fell in love with fitness as a teenager and lived through just about every workout craze known to man. Did I wear a thong leotard and do step aerobics? Yes. With a fake tan and a Playboy bunny sticker placed strategically. Was there a Tae Bo video permanently lodged in my VCR? Also yes.

Fitness people were my people. I loved eating healthy, moving my body, and figuring out how to make workouts fun. During college, I assisted and subbed in PE classes and fell even harder for it.

But somewhere along the way, it felt off.

The gym I loved closed after we found out one owner—who preached integrity like it was cardio—had been stealing members' money to buy Bitcoin. Bitcoin. Of all things. At least steal for something tangible, like a boat or a mistress. But I digress.

After that, the only job I could find was as a gym attendant at a high-end resort. And honestly? Who wouldn't want to work there? Lavender. Eucalyptus.

Citrus. If Zen had a zip code, it would be this place. Even the employee cafeteria served gourmet food. The perks were incredible.

And I gave it everything. I was an exceptional employee.

"I'm a great employee," I sobbed to no one, alone in my office, as I packed my life into the box they'd handed me.

My manager and the trainers loved me and kept offering me more responsibility, but at the end of the day, I was still picking up sweaty towels and wiping down weight machines for tourists. It was a far cry from the energy I was used to, and I could feel my passion quietly slipping away. The boredom was a slow leak, draining the joy out of something I once loved.

On my thirty-minute drive to the spa, my mind would wander. I'd imagine myself traveling—other states, other countries. I pictured long bike rides and scenic hikes, sunlight on my face instead of fluorescent gym lighting.

Sometimes I went into complete fantasy mode.

I'd see myself wandering down a cobblestone street in Italy, ducking into a café for a glass of wine and butchering the language with confidence. The chef would notice me, obviously. He'd offer me a ride on his Vespa. I'd meet his grandmother, who would kiss me on both cheeks and whisper bella, bella while scolding him in Italian.

Later—after we made love in his villa overlooking the family vineyard—he'd admit she'd told him to feed me and marry me immediately.

I mean… that could happen. Right?

Snapping back to reality as I tossed the last few things into my bag and clocked out, I realized I needed more than just a paycheck. I had had enough of the self-absorbed crowd: people with too much money, too many hours spent worrying about vanity, and zero time for genuine relationships.

I genuinely enjoyed the people, and I loved the fitness industry… until I didn't. After a few men tried to hire me for "private training," only to reveal after a couple of sessions that their real goal was a hookup, a date, or meeting someone "fit," I felt grossed out and over it.

Completely. One guy even asked me to spot him while winking. Nope. Not today, buddy.

And yet, somehow, I couldn't tear myself away. I knew I had so much more to offer. Apparently, the universe decided it was time for me to figure that out—by literally kicking me out the door.

My manager offered me ideas for other jobs.

"There is a new gym opening that needs coaches, and I need a trainer for my triathlon." She offered as she walked me to my truck.

It was sweet how she wanted to help, but in the end, she couldn't offer me my passion back, and after I told her I wasn't feeling it, she agreed that it was time for me to move forward from the fitness world and find what my next chapter would be. The loss of independence and fire had been weighing on me since Adam turned my life upside down, and I was so sick of living in that space and letting him have that power over me. It's time to try to get it back. I let myself get into a rut, spinning my wheels. I let what happened with Adam make me doubt who I am and my worth. I wanted more, and I desperately needed a change. So, I threw my stuff in the cab of my truck, hugged her, and headed out to find out what the world had in store for me. I'm Googling animal shelters now. Remember? Dog?

2 Mallory

Driving home with no plan, no answers, and no idea how I was going to pay my bills *should* have crushed me. Instead, somewhere between the freeway on-ramp and the third red light, I felt light. Almost giddy. As though someone had quietly unlocked a door I didn't know I was trapped behind.

A strange euphoria settled in. I could do whatever I wanted.

Nothing was holding me in place anymore. No schedule to obey. No expectations to meet. For the first time in a long time, everything in front of me felt wide open.

I was moving forward.

What I wanted suddenly came into focus. Freedom. Travel. New places, new people, honest conversations. My introverted instincts—usually happy to hide—were stirring. I wanted a connection. I wanted work that didn't drain me, something that felt alive and meaningful, something that let me move through the world instead of watching it pass by.

I wanted to heal from my breakup. Maybe— eventually—find love again. But not yet. That could wait.

What I couldn't wait for was my family. My brother and my aunt wouldn't say they needed me, but they did. And I needed them. I'd learned that the hard way.

This time, I wasn't building my life around a man. I was building it around the people who had never let me fall.

I've lived in this small beach town my whole life and loved it — the beaches are quaint, the weather is almost perfect (okay, 80% of the year), and the pier has my favorite restaurant-bar hybrid, *Driftwood*. The town feels "small town" even if it's technically medium-sized. I could never move away, but lately, a little wanderlust had been sneaking in.

Travel was in my blood, but money and timing had never been on my side. I'd considered going back to school—my AA degree was feeling lonely on the wall—but the cost and the time made me want to lie down in a dark room and cry. Life had other plans anyway: the natural flow, plus a breakup that still made me roll my eyes. Books weren't going to teach me what I wanted to learn.

A few weeks earlier, fueled by wine and boredom, I signed up for an online job search app. It mostly sent me absurd stuff, like today's gem: *Plastic surgeon needed in Omaha, NE.* I laughed so hard I almost snorted. Pretty sure no one wanted me wielding a scalpel on their most prized assets. I promptly put the job search on hold.

My older brother and roommate, Jackson—15 months ahead of me in life—is basically my personal cheerleader-slash-bodyguard. I mean, he didn't really have a choice. We've been living together for six years. He needed a soft landing after a messy divorce, and I needed someone to reach the top shelf for me without complaining. Win-win. He is the sweetest man on earth, and I would do anything in my power to make sure he is ok. At that time, our dad was living in assisted living, and our mom was living with our Aunt Mel in a small apartment. Dad passed shortly after that, and Mel didn't have space. Our closeness in age growing up had made us best friends. Our parents were older when they had us, and we knew we'd have to rely on each other without them at some point. At this time in our lives, neither of us was romantically involved, so it made sense for him to move in. I hadn't had a proper date in 9 months.

Jackson has this weird superpower: he can spot when I'm restless or bored before I even know it myself. He's my cheerleader for all my big ideas, my fearless protector when life gets messy, and the guy who'll bend over backward to make everyone else happy—even if it means skipping lunch. I love my big cinnamon-roll brother. Mmmm. Cinnamon rolls.

The thought of cinnamon rolls had me on a slight detour. Sweet Cheeks Bakery was just about 5 minutes out of my way, but I needed a little sugary, doughy emotional support. I parked in the small lot, and as I got out of the truck and slammed the door, I heard a tiny squeak. I looked around and saw two other cars in the lot, but no one else outside. I crouched to peer under the truck and found nothing. I heard the squeak, squeak again. Please, please don't let it be a rodent. I have an irrational fear of rodents, squirrels to be exact. I picture a squirrel jumping on me and ending up in my shirt. Just in case, I slowly peeked over the edge of my truck bed, making sure not to startle anything that might be lurking, and sure enough, there was a Clark's shoebox. The lid was on it, with holes punched out, so I couldn't see what was inside. It squeaked again. I climbed into the bed and picked up the box gently. What if it were a puppy? Could the universe be that in tune with my thoughts? I shivered. That was scary. Ok. Time to open the box.

As I lifted the lid, I heard another tiny squeak, and when I finally had the nerve to look, I saw a tiny black-and-white kitten nestled in a towel, with a lid from a plastic container and some water. Its face and body are primarily black with a white nose and paws, and a white tip on the tail. I reached in and gave it a little scratch on the head as the tiny thing mewled at me and tried to scrabble up the side of the box. It didn't look big enough to be away from its mother and was very loudly letting me know. I gently lifted it out of the box and peeked to see what the sex was. A girl. A tiny girl kitten that someone had bestowed upon me. I held her to my chest, and she began to burrow into my neck and vibrate with the tiniest purring I've ever heard. And she won my heart immediately.

There was no way I could let her go. This tiny little ball of love was a sign. A sign that everything was going to be ok. Now I just had to figure out how to tell Jackson. He had been fostering a dog for a couple of weeks, and we would have to navigate how the two would get along. My guess is great. The dog is a female Golden Retriever, and a retired service animal. She's the sweetest, chill girl, and I'm sure she will be ecstatic to have a friend to watch out for. And I don't think Jackson is going to give her up. He's been so happy since he started fostering her and will have a hard time letting her go.

Ok fine. I might be overstating the way the world works, but she is cute and definitely made me feel like someone was watching out for me. I placed her back in the box and set her inside the cab while I went inside to get my cinnamon roll. Bunny, the owner called out to me, "Malllll! It's so nice to see you! One warm gooey cinnamon roll coming up! Do you need one to go to Jackson?"

"Hi Bunny! Yes, please, go ahead and give me two extras. If Aunt Mel hears we got them without her, we'll be in trouble." I'm pretty sure her real name isn't Bunny, but that's all I've ever known. Mel says everyone called her that in junior high because she could beat everyone on track and field day, including the boys. So, it just stuck.

"You got it! Coming right up! And grab yourself a cup of coffee if you want it. The yummy creamer you like is in the little fridge under the counter." I hear her call from the kitchen. "What were you up to in the truck bed out there? Looked serious. Everything ok with the truck? Should I call B?" Her husband, Barry, was a mechanic and had helped me with so many things on the truck over the years.

He and Bunny had been friends with my parents since they were in junior high school together. He has worked on the car for years, even before it was mine; he helped my dad keep it running in tip-top condition. The thing about all of my parents' friends is that they were generous people. They were the kind of people who never hesitated to offer a hand or a cup of coffee. They genuinely care for everyone in their orbit, as long as they weren't dicks. They didn't allow dicks in the circle. I needed to come in here more often.

"The truck is fine, but you'll never believe my morning."

And I tell her everything about how I think it happened because I secretly wanted it. I tell her that a brilliant and kind angel left me this sweet kitten.

Bunny listened like a saint. Customers came and went, but she didn't interrupt once. "Grab a coffee, folks. Give me a minute," she called over her shoulder.

When I finished, she let out a big sigh and took my hands in hers. "Sweet Mallory, your heart is as pure as fresh-fallen snow. Losing your job seems like a speed bump, but I believe it's a break in the storm for you. It may look messy from the edges, but if you keep moving, things are clearing up. You took that job because you had to. Now, you have the chance to do something new. I can't tell you what or when, but trust me — it's going to be great. Something big is coming."

Her smile is infectious. Even through my teary eyes, I can't help but grin.

The kitten, who had been staring at Bunny like she was a wizard, suddenly launched itself at my sleeve, hanging on like a furry little paratrooper. "Hey!" I yelp, trying not to trip over the bag of cinnamon rolls. Bunny laughs.

"Now go take care of that little menace while I get back to work and feed these people," she says, still giggling. She squeezes my hands one last time.

I grab the cinnamon rolls, scoop up the kitten, and wave goodbye. "Tell Barry 'Hey' for me, okay?" The kitten meows like it's agreeing, and Bunny waves back, still glowing.

She waves and gives a thumbs-up. "Give Mel and Jackson a squeeze for us."

So, with my windows down, letting the warm air soothe me, and Whitney Houston blaring on the stereo in my 2005 F-150 truck inherited from my dad, I tried to focus on what the future held. I heard a lot of jokes about driving this truck. But I loved it. It made me feel like I was living in a different time, totally unconcerned with what anyone thought about it, or even whether it was new or flashy enough to get someone's attention. If a guy were going to be interested in me, it wouldn't be because I could make a huge car payment. The kitten slept peacefully in her box that was resting against my leg as I scratched under her little chin. "What should I call you, little cutie?" And the shoebox spoke to me. Clark. Her name is Clark. "We are going to make this work, Clark. Aren't we? You and I against the world!" She mewled and stretched, and I laughed. I'd take that as a yes. I think Bunny was right, things were going to be ok.

When I sped around the corner, I saw it. A beacon in the shape of an airstream travel trailer with a for-sale sign taped in the window called out to me. My heart leapt at the flood of memories of growing up and the many trips we took, and even just backyard campouts when my dad didn't have enough days off to go far. Not just any airstream, but an Argosy. There weren't many of these made, and we had one growing up. We named her "Arlene". Sadly, my parents had to sell her when we were in high school to pay some bills.

I slowed quickly to a stop to see what they were asking for. From the outside, it looked to be in good condition for its age. The paint on the outside was peeling, but as I looked through the windows, I saw it needed a little love and elbow grease on the inside, and my heart was racing. Could this be a sign from the universe? Could Bunny have predicted that the little dream brewing in my heart could be the realization right here on the side of the highway with an old trailer? I've always wanted to own one of these again, but for a different purpose than camping. The sign in the window had a phone number and said $25,000 OBO. I inhaled sharply. That was a lot of money. I had a little savings and some cash that my dad had given me before he died. Maybe I could make an offer, but I'd have to lowball it since I'd need some money to fix it up. But what the hell? In minutes, I was in the car calling the number. What's the worst thing that could happen? They could say no, and I moved on with my life. Whatever that looked like. What do you think, Clark? Should we see if this is our destiny? "Mew." She responded, stretching and beginning to lick her tiny paw. "Ok. I'll take that as a 'yes'. Let's do it. Fingers crossed." And I crossed her paw and my fingers and tapped out the numbers.

"Hello?" a gruff voice answers. There is a lot of background noise. It sounds like a party or a busy street. This guy did not sound like a man ready to haggle, much less take a lowball offer. I imagined him sitting in the back room of a dive bar, grouchy about having to sell his prized possession to pay his ex-wife alimony.

Snapped back to reality, but another gruff, albeit louder, "HELLO?"

I cleared my throat, nerves starting to get to me. "Hi, um, yes, I was calling about the travel trailer for sale.

I…UH…have…er… would like to offer $15,000." I knew I probably sounded like a teenager trying to buy a skateboard, and it was so low, but I needed a little cash to make the changes that I'm sure would cost, plus licenses and fees to run a food establishment, plus hiring help to make it my own and make my dream come true.

A resounding peal of laughter rings through the phone, but no response from the gruff voice at the other end. Oh, God. What have I got myself into? But I muster up some courage and listen to Bunny's voice, cheering me on.

I scramble into negotiating mode, which I really have no business doing, and start rambling, trying to sound confident.

"Now, I know it's an Argosy, and I recognize the value, but I really need to do something crazy, and this little old girl of a trailer is exactly what I need. She needs some lovin' just like me. (Fuck, why did I say THAT?) Anyway,"

I continue, "It must be fate or kismet or whatever. I just got fired, my savings are sad, and my Auntie Mel is probably going to kill me for buying it. I haven't had a proper date in 8 months because they are all fish bros, you know? Well, probably not. But I need a distraction, you know, something to keep me busy. At least it's not a dog! Amirite? Um.. So, I've always had this idea to have an adult frozen lemonade stand called 'Squeeze the Day'."

I hear the words coming out of my mouth, and I think I should stop. But I don't stop. I lean in.

"Oh, I don't mean 'adult' like porn, I mean like adult beverages, like alcohol. Um, not that I have anything against porn, per se. If you like porn, that's fine; I won't judge you. It seems a bit unrealistic to me, you know? From what I've seen, I mean. I'm not an aficionado. I've only dabbled, out of curiosity. Not that you asked. But anyway, no porn. But I understand if you don't think it's a good deal for you. Maybe consider it an investment in a fellow human who needs a little adventure and wants to see what's out there. Me, that's me I'm talking about in case that was confusing. And I'm really trying just to take my own advice and SEIZE the day. Get It? I…"

3 Jake

"STOP!" I growl. *How did this woman know it was an Argosy?* I think. Not many people knew that, and it was such a special piece of history for my best friend and me. I felt a little twinge in my chest just at the thought of it. We had so many family trips in that trailer—the many road trips up the coast. Dad was making us sing "Row Your Boat" in the round, and Mom, never able to stay on the right verse, made us laugh until tears were streaming down our cheeks. The campgrounds were always full of other families, and we all organically decided to hang out together. I have a vague memory of other families having the same trailer we did, and our dads talking incessantly about how amazing it was. They even started making plans to start an Argosy club. All the kids hung out and played games until long after dark, and for an only child, this was especially meaningful. The campfires, fishing, s'mores, and crazy fun games are all still at the forefront of my precious memories.

Snapping back to reality, realizing I had checked out for a minute, and hearing silence. Did I come off too harshly? That definitely wasn't my intention. So many unexpected thoughts and emotions were running through me right now. I'm now realizing that selling the trailer is creating a visceral response. I hold so much of my childhood in those memories. The feelings of those memories mixed with the sadness of letting this piece of our history go, and I don't know what to do with them. Can I really do this? I don't hear anything on the other end of the phone except the sound of a kitten mewing loudly.

"Hello? Are you still there?" I say, calming my voice, and now with the background a little quieter. "I'm sorry I had to step into my office so I could hear you." Did I hear a cat? This phone call was getting weird.

There is a long silence.

"Oh, YES. I'm still here. I'm sorry for the rambl…" the woman squeaks, and before she can start up again,

"I'll take the offer." I cut her off mid-word.

"Fuck me sideways!! You what? Yes? Oh my god! Thank you!" her voice peals over the phone. I imagine this woman doing a little happy dance right there on the side of the road, and it makes my lips quirk into a smile.

"Uh…well…you're welcome." I say with an amused chuckle, the gruffness softened, "I'll have my accountant get in touch with you. Is this the best number to reach you?"

We set appointments to talk with my accountant and to meet with them for the title. Who is this girl, and why is her voice now stuck in my brain?

4 Mallory

I hang up and cannot help myself. "Clark! Did you hear that? We just got ourselves a new project in the shape of an awesome trailer!" She mews loudly and turns to snuggle into her box. I woop and jump up and down until I realize I'm on the side of the highway and cars are slowing to see if I'm ok. I'm not ok; I've just started making my dreams come true.

Okay, maybe "rash decision" is an understatement— definitely rash. Auntie Mel would have strong opinions. I just lost my job, adopted a cat, and bought a beat-up trailer—all in a couple of hours. I mean, what else do you do when you're trying to heal from a breakup *and* get laid off?

Mel worried I'd end up on a hamster wheel forever, chasing things that didn't make me happy. After my ex hurt me so badly, she assumed I hated love and wanted nothing to do with relationships. Honestly, maybe she wasn't wrong.

Hopefully, she'd understand and be supportive. But that was a problem for later. She would surely love Clark, and I was banking that the nostalgia of the trailer would win her over.

I open the group chat with Jackson and Aunt Mel.**ME:** Heyyy. So, I've got a few things to share.

Aunt Mel: This sounds ominous. Should we have dinner, or are you just going to tell us now?

Jackson: I swear to God if you and Adam got back together, I'm locking you out.

Me: OMG. JACKSON! First of all, it's my house. Second, ew. I would absolutely never in 800 bazillion years get back together with that lying, cheating piece of shit. Do not ever say that again. Why would you even think that?

Jackson: Ok, sorry. ☹ I just freaked. You usually don't like surprises.

Me: Ok. Dinner or now? You guys pick.

Aunt Mel: I can't wait. Tell me now. Then dinner to hash it out if needed.

Me: Fine.

    ...

Jackson: Hello? The suspense is killing me.

Me: Sorry. The kitten had to pee.

Aunt Mel: The what, now?

Jackson: Aww! You got Wanda a friend!

Me: I'm so happy you feel that way. She's adorable and so sweet. Her name is Clark. I think Wanda will be pleased with her sister from another mister.

Aunt Mel: Ok, well, as long as this isn't taking the place of a man?

Me: Aunt Mel! Geez. It's a pet. Men are not pets. And I'm not ready for a man. Anyway... there's more.

Aunt Mel: …

Jackson: …

Me: I lost my job.

Jackson: Oh no! I'm so sorry! What happened?

Me: They're restructuring the spa and fitness team. Business is slow. Last in, first out. So… that's me.

Aunt Mel: Well, that sucks. Are you ok with money?

Me: Well, yes. I still have what Dad left me and some other savings. But…

Aunt Mel: Oh no. But what? Did you buy stocks or a timeshare?

Me: I bought—*sends picture of trailer*

Jackson: What the…? Is that like the one we had as kids? But why? What's it for? It's kind of… beat up.

Aunt Mel: Oh my. Yeah. Let's have dinner. Come over at 5.

Me: Ok. I'll bring dinner. Text me what you want from Marty's.

Next, I dial one of my best friends. I needed to hear a friendly voice. And Charley is the sweetest, most supportive person on earth. I need some honest-to-goodness good vibes.

"You did WHAT?" Charley exclaims.

"You heard me correctly. I bought a trailer. I admit, I didn't completely think it through. You know, I've always wanted to do something that would let me travel and set my own schedule. I guess I didn't think about what it was going to take to get me there. I saw this old trailer on the road, all lonely and well, for sale. I don't know. Something just called out. Like it was meant to be." And I say quieter, "And I got a kitten." I prepare to defend this impulsive moment.

"Mal, a kitten? Oh my god. What are you doing? Ok, let's talk about this. What kind of money do you have to put into it? How much will the changes cost? And, a kitten?" She replied.

"Well, I'm not completely sure. I know it's out of the blue crazy. But I think the painting and general stuff might be pretty affordable. But I didn't think about putting in a serving window. I guess that's crucial for a food truck.

That might be pretty pricey. And, I didn't mean to get a kitten. Someone put it in my truck, and well, I think we need each other. And what was I supposed to do, just dump iy? No. I couldn't. So, Kitten." I cringe and then snap a quick picture of Clark and I snuggled up and send it.

She sighs, "Girl. You are so crazy. I love the idea. Aww. Clark is darling. And yes, probably good for you right now. I think it's great, actually." She pauses. "So, back to the trailer. I'm thinking, maybe you, me, and Whit can team up and make it a group effort. Of course, we have jobs so that the work part would be yours, but I would love to invest in you, friend."

"What?" My eyes go wide in shock, "You want to buy in? Be a partner? That would be fucking amazing! I'm so overwhelmed. I had no expectations when I called. I just wanted to share my excitement, and look what happened! You are the best!"

"Let's set up a Zoom with Whitney. I know she's got some money set aside from her car accident settlement. I think this might be something fun for us to do together, and maybe when you make it a huge success, which you will, we will all be set for life."

I laugh, "Ok, let's not get ahead of ourselves."

"Says the girl who just up and bought a decrepit trailer with no funds to fix it up," she snarks.

"How dare you talk about our girl that way! She isn't decrepit. She's well-loved. Do you want me to call you decrepit when you get old?" I defend.

"No, no. Ok. OUR girl, huh? Let's set that call and see what we come up with. Meanwhile, find out what the service door will cost." She laughs.

I nod even though she can't see me. "Yes. I'm on it. Oh my gosh, Charley! I'm even more excited than I was before! Text me with times and give me a couple of days to get the quotes."

"Ok, girl. I need to go. Oh, and Mal?" she says.

"Yeah?"

"Don't go buying big purchases on your own anymore. You have at least one business partner now." She commands.

"EEEEE! I CANNOT wait! Thank you, Charley. You are amazing, and the best friend a girl could ask for."

I didn't have many great friendships growing up, so this rang truer than they even knew. We moved in the area a few times, so I was forced to change schools. Even though we never went too far, I always seemed to be the new girl wherever I was and had to navigate new relationships.

Not everyone was receptive to a new person. It gave me the confidence to believe it was worth being my friend. Kids can be pretty brutal at times, though, and for no reason. As I got older, I learned that they were most likely trying to navigate their own insecurities, and that was how they did it. They thought they were funny by being mean, and other insecure kids followed because they didn't know any better. It made me so grateful for the few amazing friends I did keep over the years. Charley and Whitney were definitely at the top of a very short list. Their place was secure in my heart, whether or not they could help me financially. Just knowing that they were willing to try to make my crazy dreams come true solidified my love for them.

Later that week, we connected on a video call and talked about everything, from our history to how meaningful this would be to us and our futures. I was able to locate a local guy who modifies and customizes cars and trailers. He had done another modification of an Airstream for a couple I worked with at the resort and was willing to work with our budget. The budget that I made up on the spot because I didn't prepare for him to ask me. Completely clueless, I said $6000, and he came back with $7000. I brought the number to the girls, and they were both prepared to pitch in $5000 each. My heart swelled with love for them and their generosity. They each gave me $3k, and I was able to splurge on better exterior paint and a fancier logo design with the money in my savings account. And get all the inspections and permits I hadn't planned for.

Now I'm going to smooth things over with my family. Deep breaths. It's going to be fine. Everything is fine.

5 Mallory

Marty's is a Mediterranean spot we all love right around the corner from Mel's. They have the best kabobs and even better Baklava.

"I'm here!" I call out, but don't see anyone in the house.

"We're back here. We already have drinks set up." Aunt Mel calls from the back patio.

I plop Marty's bags on the table and look up to see them both sitting with their feet up, cocktails in hand, staring at me in confusion, wanting a full explanation for our text conversation. "Give me a sec. I got Sweet Cheeks

Cinnamon rolls, too." I sing out. "And Clark is in the truck. Let me go grab them."

Jackson squeals, actually squeals. "You brought Clark AND cinnamon rolls. My life is complete! Let me give my new cat-niece some scritches immediately."

I grin. Jackson is so easy to please. I knew I could count on him to love all my crazy shenanigans. What a love.

Just as expected, Jackson and Wanda adore Clark. After a few minutes of sniffing and general confusion, they became fast friends. Clark snuggled under Wanda's front leg, and they both slept peacefully while Ant Mel grilled me on my plans.

I explain to them the way the whole day went down, complete with finding Clark and the phone call with the Grumpy man—my hero who sold me the trailer and is making my dreams come true.

"Who is this guy? Is he local?" Jackson presses me.

"I don't think so. Maybe he's selling it for someone else, or it's like an inheritance thing or something. We didn't get that deep. I was just overwhelmed that he would sell it so cheaply. He wasn't exactly chatty."

"Yeah, that's crazy, but how lucky for you. This is what you wanted: a fun way to travel and meet new people." He nudges me.

"Maybe you should meet him. You like grumpy men. Maybe you can bring a little sunshine to his life?" Mel chimes in, giving her eyebrows a wiggle.

"Um, no Mel. I'm not trying to date the random stranger who sold me the trailer. That's some crazy talk. I doubt we even need to meet in person. He said his accountant would handle everything. So, stop trying to matchmake me with anything male and breathing."

I have earned the right to be picky, and Mel knows it. She wants me to be cared for, and I know she has my best interest at heart, but I refuse to go out with just anyone. My standards are high after Adam. And that's that. My heart is too fragile, and I want more. I NEED more from a partner.

They resolve to support my endeavors. Jackson has already upgraded himself to Clark's stepfather, and I think Wanda is fine with her new sister from another mister. He agreed that she will be well cared for whenever I am busy or traveling. I can't help but feel completely fine and content with my family and now my new cat daughter. I get up to leave and scoop her up from Wanda's clutch. She gives a little whimper and a big doggie kiss to her head. "Aww," we say in unison. What a day.

6 Mallory

I worked, with the help of Jackson and a few friends, for six months scrubbing, ripping out the old interior, and preparing the trailer for the window installation. It took about 6 months, which was 6 months faster than I had imagined. I was ready to Door Dash to earn some cash to get me by, but the work just all fell into place just in time. I could handle the business end and take care of Clark without doing any outside work.

"Finally finished!" I squealed and spun around in the tiny space. I took a last swipe at the counters and straightened the sign on the wall that said "Where Troubles Melt Like Lemon Drops" - my nod to my love of all things Wizard of Oz, and gave the lemon-yellow curtains a swish to make them lie uniformly. She was a 'beaut', as my dad used to proudly proclaim after waxing the car. Mom would stand at the front door and call out to him, "Woohoo! She sure is." She didn't care at all about the car, but she was his biggest hype woman for sure. Times like these made me miss them so much. I really would love for them to see this dream come true. Therefore, this called for a celebration. I typed out a text to my brother.

Mal: She's ready! Drinks at Driftwood?

Almost immediately, a response popped up.

Jackson: Fuck YES! When can I see her?

Mal: Now! I'll drag her home first. Meet me there, and then we can walk to the restaurant.

Jackson: Perfect.

Driving with my little sweet lemon behind me made me so happy, and watching people on the road take a second look gave me such pride. I cannot wait to open her up at my first event.

We meet at my house, and when Jackson pulls in, he barely takes time to park the car before he jumps out to head towards me. As he walks my way, I'm struck by how much he looks like our father. He's ruggedly handsome but in a very laid-back and unassuming way. He got my dad's disarming blue eyes and dark auburn hair and keeps a very trim beard. He's not tall, maybe 5'11, but built like a Muscle Man toy. My heart tugs at the reminder.

"I can't believe you finished it! It seems like just a minute ago you were telling us about it." Jackson says, pulling me out of my reminiscing when he reaches me and picks me up, swinging me in a circle. I'm laughing. "I know!! Ok, put me down, crazy man!"

I give him the grand tour of the trailer, and I'm so proud. I had the exterior painted a bright, shiny lemon yellow on the bottom panels and white on the top panels and roof. I lined the windows with lights that can change color with the seasons or remain bright white. The wheels are actual white walls, and the trim and bumpers are painted white. The heating and AC unit has a decal that makes it look like a giant lemon slice. The name on the side, "Squeeze the Day," is in a large, retro-funky font with an orange-and-yellow overlay. The interior features a service counter and a bar area stocked with locally made vodka, gin, and tequila in various flavors. I decided to keep the bathroom intact and working for emergencies at events or on the road. A large fridge freezer lines the back wall, along with four industrial blenders for fresh service. I plan to have a lot of ready-made options for speed and ease, and to cut down on the amount of fresh fruit I have to carry with me, but making something fresh is always a possibility.

We head over to Driftwood, our favorite restaurant. It's one of the only places with an ocean view and good, affordable food. They have stellar cocktails, and the people who work there seem well taken care of and enjoy themselves, which makes for an excellent customer experience.

We ordered our fish tacos, which we think are the best in the world. They make them with a jalapeno batter that is beyond amazing. Jackson gets a beer, and I order a lemon drop martini. I usually would have a glass of Rosé, but I felt like drinking something fancy to celebrate in style, and we ordered two green tea shots to have a little fun. We clink our shot glasses and drain them in style. "To Mallory and new adventures!" He shouts, and I cannot stop the giant smile on my face. I have no idea what to expect or where this will go, but I'm committed to trying. I have to make this work.

"Remember all the crazy stuff dad used to set up on our camping trips?" Jackson reminisces, thinking about the trailer we had as kids.

"Oh my god, how could I forget? The way he would recruit other dads around the campground and have those elaborate scavenger hunts and contests? No one could say no to him." I laugh. "He and Mom were just so likable. Mom and her amazing muumuus!"

He folds over laughing, "Oh man, do you remember the year she brought multiple muumuus and got as many of the moms and even a couple of dads to dress up and have a fashion show? I never laughed so hard at that one, Dad with the big beard who could barely get his huge arms into the dress."

"Oh yes! And the kids had to rate them like a beauty pageant. God, what freaking fun times we had. They would be so proud of you, Mal. I feel like they are part of this, even though they aren't with us."

"I miss them." We both say it at the same time, then lift our glasses again: "To mom and dad!"

He sets his glass down and bites his lip. It's his tell that he wants to say something but feels uncomfortable or nervous about it. He's done it since I can remember, and it is so endearing I can't help but put him out of his misery. "What?" I prod my finger into his shoulder. "You have that look like you need to say something. Out with it."

He shrugs, "I just want to save you some annoying conversations with Aunt Mel. You know she's going to see this as you running away from relationships and falling in love."

"Oh my god." I groan. "I'm not running. I'm just strategically avoiding any entanglements with lying cheaters." I turn to him with a large cheesy smile.

"You're adorable and funny. You know she wants you happy and to heal. You have not been the same since Adam, and you know it. You're skittish and reserved, and that is not the Mallory I grew up with." He argues

"Ok, you're right. I have been avoiding anything to do with putting myself back out there. It's hard, Jackson. You know. You've been hurt, too. Putting your heart out there is scary. Are you ready to jump into the dating pool again?" I ask

"Not really. But my situation is different. I was married, and there was no cheating going on. We just got married too young, and it wasn't what we really wanted. Truthfully, we did it for mom, and that was a mistake. You are discounting ALL men because of one bad seed."

"You weren't there. You didn't see what I saw. Adam told me I was his everything forever. And then decided to use another woman as a sock puppet in my bedroom." I cringe, nervously rubbing my hands on my glass.

His hands go up in surrender. "Ok, ok. That's an image I can do without. I know it was awful. HE is the absolute worst and should be tortured with red ants in his boxers. But he is not all men. I know that Aunt Mel only wants to see you happy and settled. She is not going to think this trailer is leading you to that. I need to prepare you for what she's going to come at you with."

"Ok. I understand. I will be prepared. And you know, I'll put ONE dating app back on my phone. You can tell her that. Maybe that will appease her." I had grown tired of the dating apps with the ghosting and the endless line of "fish bros" one after another. Don't you know what a fish bro is? Oh well, let me regale you. There appears to be a trend among men on dating apps who post pictures of themselves holding a fish. Why? Who the fuck knows? I have often wanted to match with them and have a date to find out what it means. I suspect that they don't even know. It's a trap!

He laughs and shakes his head, "Yeah. I'll let her know. Weirdo."

"So, what's your first event? Have you found anything? A carnival? Party? You want me to get all the boys together and have a big grand opening over at the Y?" Jackson asks. I laugh, "Um, I don't think an adult beverage event is the type of thing the local YMCA is looking for."

Jackson is the Director at the YMCA in Ventura, and he knows everyone in town. If you live here, you either have or have had a membership to the Y. He's just one of those people that everyone loves and would do almost anything for.

"Well, I have an acquaintance who wants me to set up at her mom's birthday bash. It's at the tennis park, and I think it will be a great place to get some exposure and maybe hand out some cards." I say. "Then I'm going to a networking event in San Diego. It's pretty exclusive, and not many trucks get to be part of it. I put in an application on a whim, and I think they invited me because my idea is unique. I'm really hoping this will get me some connections with other restaurants and events I could pull up at. You're still good to watch Clark this weekend?"

As he nods, my phone rings. I glanced at the screen. "Whit." Weird. Shouldn't she be at work, I mused? Girlfriend was a workaholic and barely had time to answer a text most days, much less call, so it must be important. I answered, about to say something witty and sassy because that's what I do best, but Whitney started speaking immediately. "Charley isn't doing well. Can you get away?"

"Oh shit." I don't even need to ask what is going on; I know I need to be there for her. "I'm already planning to be in San Diego with Amarilla at an event (I named my trailer 'yellow' in Spanish because she's so beautifully sunny and 'yellow' just wasn't sassy enough) this weekend, but I can head down a couple of days early. I'll get us a Suite at La Locanda and meet you there." "Perfect," she responded. "I'll pick up snacks." Whit doesn't go anywhere without snacks.

The next morning, I showered and packed for the week. I didn't have much information about what to wear for the event, so I packed some cute summery pieces, a few sundresses, and, of course, bikinis. If I knew my girls at all, we would be going to the beach and the pool at least a couple of times.

As I grabbed my favorite bikini from the drawer, I spied my bright pink vibrator. I stared at it for just a moment, then shook my head. There wouldn't be time for that, right? I thought. I turned, then paused. Why not have it, just in case? I quickly turned back and grabbed it, slamming the drawer shut and shoving it into the bottom of my bag. Always be prepared, I smiled.

We made plans to meet at the hotel, and after giving Clark some final head kisses and chin scritches, and after a quick stop at the coffee shop drive-thru, I was on the road, iced latte in hand. I cued up my Love Bites podcast and was on my way.

Season 3: Episode 35 Chance Encounters and Back Seat Blow Jobs

Sara: So today we're talking about Chance encounters and backseat blow jobs. Can they lead to forever love?

Blake: (Laughing) Are we talking about this today because of your encounter today? With a hot sauna guy? Ohhh, Sara, you're blushing!! Are you in loooove!?

Sara: (Squeals) Ahhhh! I don't know. How could I be? Should I tell the story?

Blake: For god's sake, woman, tell the story! That's what we came for – no pun intended. Buckle up, Love Biters, this is a good one!!

Sara: Ok, here we go! And just as a disclaimer, this is not for children, so unless you want to have an unplanned conversation about sex with your kids, turn it off or get them out of the room!

Ok, let's go!

7 JAKE

I'm sitting at the bar at the Driftwood in Ventura. I don't get up this way much. The staff at this location is top-notch and really takes care of business. I know that I can usually just set up a video chat with the manager and things will get taken care of. I tried to come up once every six months to chat, check the location, give them a thumbs-up in person, make any necessary changes, and call it a day.

So, why did I decide to stay overnight this time? Was it because I knew the woman who bought my trailer lived in the area, and my curiosity was killing me? Maybe. But I couldn't just call her up and tell her I needed to meet the woman who now owns a piece of my family history.

Right? That would be weird. I don't even know her name. I've officially lost it. Did I think I would just randomly run into someone and voila! It would be her. God, I'm stupid and desperate. I can't get it out of my head.

So, I order a beer and sit at the end of the bar, considering my options. Just then, a couple sits at the other end of the bar. They appear to be celebrating something. She's gorgeous and looks so happy, like she just won the life lottery. I should send them a drink. I wonder if they are together. I ask the bar back, Tristan, if he knows. Maybe they are locals.

He tells me he's pretty sure they are brother and sister. They come in often.

Excellent. I wait a bit until they have almost finished their drinks and send them the same. They look over, and I hold up my beer. "It looked like you were celebrating something. So, congratulations on whatever it is. My friend Tristan tells me you two are locals and come in often. We appreciate your business.

"Thank you!" they say in unison. The male raises his glass, "My sister here just started her own business! She is realizing a long-time dream. So, thanks for the congrats."

She lifts her glass, and our eyes meet. Her lashes flutter, her cheeks turn pink, and her mouth opens slightly. I think she is going to speak, but she smiles and takes a drink. She mouths thank you as her phone rings. She answers the call as she goes outside. I want to talk to her. Talking to a local, I can find the girl with the trailer or get a lead. But she comes right back, grabs her purse and jacket, and takes one more sip. She tells her brother she has to go and gives him a quick peck on the cheek. And she is gone. The brother slams his drink and throws a couple of bills on the counter. He gives me a final wave, "Thanks again, man!"

I lift my hand in a non-committal wave and slump down. This is ridiculous. I should go home. Everything doesn't happen for a reason, and I fucking hate that phrase. Shit happens, and we move forward in life. Some of that is excellent stuff, and some sucks. Some events we have choices and some we don't, but don't ever tell me everything leads to something else. I thank Tristan and cancel my hotel.

My best friend since we were 6 years old, and his family moved in next door, likes to say this to get under my skin, but now, he REALLY thinks this is it. The REAL "everything happens for a reason" moment. Let me tell you why.

We decided to meet in San Diego for a last-minute weekend fun trip. Aforementioned, best friend Sam has a younger sister Ivy (who goes by Ivy Jane on stage, because Jane is their mom's name, who passed away from cancer 5 years ago). She is an up-and-coming pop star and has a gig at the San Diego County Fairgrounds opening for some larger act. So, we decided to go check it out. Plus, I have a work event in the area, so the timing is perfect.

Both of us are doing reasonably well financially and have had no issue taking a few days off. I own several popular bars/restaurants in Southern California, and Sam runs a production company in Los Angeles. So, we decided to splurge a little and stay at La Locanda. It's a 5-star resort, with all the rooms overlooking the beach, a full-service spa, fine dining, and an amazing little bar that's perfect to tuck away with friends or schmooze clients, or have a gin and tonic and their fried lobster bites because I can.

Running five restaurants can be very stressful, and I was looking forward to some serious downtime, even if it was only for a weekend. I scheduled a massage and hoped to have some cocktails by the pool. As we made the plan, I could already feel the promise of relaxation changing my attitude.

The drive was awful, so I decided to call my mom to kill some time.

Her sweet voice comes through the receiver, "Hello?"

"Hey, Mom. What are you up to?" I ask.

"Jakey! Hi, honey. Oh, Dad and I are just heading out to play pickleball. What are you up to?"

I laugh. My parents have become obsessed with pickleball and even joined a league for those 55 and older. Although mom likes to remind everyone that she's "barely 55".

"Oh, great. I'm glad you're getting it in. I'm just heading to San Diego and stuck in traffic. Just thought I'd check in."

"You're on speaker in the car, sweetie. Dad's here."

"Hey, son. What's in San Diego?" he chimes in.

"Oh, just that networking event I put on last year. And, Sam and I are meeting up a couple of days early to hang out and go to Ivy Jane's concert."

"Aw, Sammy! Tell him we love him," Mom interjects.

"Jake, don't work too hard. Life isn't just filling the bank account, you know?", Dad says.

"I know, Dad. I'm trying. That's why we are going a couple of days early. I'm even going to see if I can get a massage.", I say.

"OOOO, nice. Where are you staying?" Mom asks.

"La Locanda", I tell her.

"Oh, Jake, that's lovely. Remember camping up in that area? I think you were about 12. Such a beautiful beach," she reminisces.

I cringe slightly, knowing how much they didn't want to let go of the trailer, but made the hard decision to allow Jake to sell it. I think they still wish they could have kept it, but no one had used it in so long, and it really needed work. "Yes, Mom. That was awesome. We have some awesome memories from those days. For sure."

"Ok, Jakey, we're at the courts now, so we gotta get going. We love you lots. Give Sam and Ivy squeezes and remember to relax!", she calls into the speaker.

"Ok, mom. Love you guys, too. Be careful out there. Don't get injured," I tell them.

They laugh, "Oh, we're the young ones in the crowd. I think we're ok. Ok. Bye." And the line goes silent. Well, that killed about 10 minutes.

Taking on the traffic on a Wednesday afternoon during the first weekend of the fair was not a bright idea, and a trip that usually took about an hour was closer to 2 hours. We didn't need to be there that early in the week. I had a corporate event on Friday, and Ivy Jane was playing on Saturday, so we decided to go early to unwind a bit before then. We would normally room together, but Sam mentioned he might have a visitor, which was not an option. "Man, I have been seeing this girl for a month, and she's amazing, smart, and kind, and so SO hot, which doesn't hurt. If I can get her to meet me in San Diego, too, this might be the night. (waggles eyebrows) If you know what I mean."

"Jesus, Sam." I say, "Everyone knows what you mean. But honestly, I'm happy for you." Unfortunately, there is no prospect for me. I haven't dated anyone seriously in about a year, and after the last girl smashed my heart to bits, the prospect doesn't interest me. Unfortunately, I do still have the voice of that girl who bought the trailer in my head. Her rambling and mention of porn did things to me that I vaguely remembered as being turned on, but I had no idea who she was or even what she looked like. I do recall her saying something about unrealistic, and yeah, that's what I always thought, too. That stuff CANNOT be real. Why am I even thinking about this?

If I really wanted to track her down, I had the information at my disposal, but that would be inappropriate. Right? And also, what the actual fuck? Am I going to hit up a girl I spoke with for precisely 3 minutes last year? Absolutely not. There are more fish in the sea, as they say. Although I'm really obsessed with finding this one fish that I know zero about.

But for the sake of Sam's love life, thankfully, they had two rooms available, being such a busy time in the area. There would be no sock-on-the-door moments this weekend.

We checked into our rooms and decided to meet up at 6 for cocktails and dinner in the hotel restaurant. As we were walking away, I stopped to talk to the concierge. "Do you have any massage appointments available for the morning?" This is where things went off the rails, although I didn't know it at the time. The smiling man said yes, they had one appointment at 8:30 am, and asked if I would like it. I booked it even though it was a little earlier than I would like, but figured it would be good to get started with a nice, long massage.

As I turned to leave, I hadn't noticed a line forming behind me and slammed into the most beautiful girl I had ever seen. I feel something like a bolt of electricity - like a static shock - run up my spine as I look down at her. A flash of familiarity strikes me. I feel like I have seen this woman before. Her reddish-brown hair is piled into a messy bun. She has a soft scent of lavender and something that smells like a plant I can't recall the name of. She had on a bright pink tank top and cut-off jean shorts, and may or may not have been wearing a bra. I'm really trying not to look long enough to make a decision. But as I dragged my eyes over her fantastic body, I could see the slight protrusion of hardened nipples, making me think no, definitely no bra— eyes up, Jake. Dear god, she was hot. She was petite and had clearly worked out enough to give her arms and legs a chiseled look. She had chocolate-brown eyes, a cute, slightly turned-up nose, and a perfectly shaped bow mouth. That mouth. Captivating. I've seen that mouth before. But when?

Her eyes went wide, and she apologized profusely. "Oh, I am SO sorry. A typical case of looking at my phone and not paying attention to where I am going. Amirite? I mean, can I just put this thing away and focus? People these days and their electronics are just the worst. I hope you can forgive me for being such a klutz. I'm not usually like this." She laughs.

I stutter. "It's fine." And she's got her hand on my chest, fingers spread wide. I swear she squeezed my pec for just a second, then quickly clapped her hand over her mouth.

"Sorry for touching your pecs, um.. squeezing you. Ugh. Hands off!" She says, holding her hands up and looking mortified.

We both try to leave, and neither of us can decide who is going right or left. I hold her by the shoulder and gently guide her to one side.

I can smell a faint sweetness of wine on her breath. Looks like she's had a little fun at lunch. Her cheeks are slightly rosy, probably from the mixture of sun and alcohol. I'm staring at her mouth as she talks, and I freeze because something about her voice rings a bell. It's weirdly familiar. No, there's no way. Why? How could we end up in the same place again? Ok, Jake, pull it together, I chastise myself. I'm imagining things. There is no way it's her. Move on.

"It's fine. No harm done." I say as I begin to walk away, I hear the concierge say, "Yes, miss, your 8:30 reservation for your massage is confirmed. Please arrive 15 minutes early to have a tour". For a moment, I think, *Wow, we're getting a massage at the same time, too.* But it's just a coincidence. The universe doesn't work like that. I'll likely never see her again. And it's probably for the best. I haven't set myself up to make lasting relationships. And then words come out of my mouth toward the back of her head.

"Hey, I have a massage appointment at that time as well. Maybe I'll see you there?"

She doesn't realize I'm talking to her at first and doesn't acknowledge me. So I tap her on the shoulder. What am I doing? This woman is going to deck me. I'm a stranger talking to her and now touching her. In my defense, she touched me first. She squeezed my pec.

She startles a bit at my touch, turning quickly. "What? Oh, huh?"

"I...uh...I'm sorry. I just overheard you were going to the spa at the same time. Thought maybe we would cross paths again. You know, it's weird, I feel like I know you."

"Yeah, you shouldn't go around touching random strangers. I don't think we've met." She winks. "I think we will be on different sides of the spa. You know, men and women?" She gestures, pointing back and forth between us.

"Ah, yes. I'm a man. You're a woman." And yes, I'm aware I sound like a freaking caveman. I've got to get out of here. I clearly have no game. And as I said, I'm not in the market for a relationship.

"Ok, well. Sorry again for startling you." And I turn to leave. Humiliated.

I need a drink.

8 Mallory

I'm waiting in line to check on my massage appointment and make sure I can park my trailer in the back lot until after dinner, when I can take it to the convention center to set up. The event is on Friday, but I can set up my trailer at the venue up to 2 days early if needed. The girls head up to get settled in our room.

Charley and Whitney had been my best friends since high school. They moved to the Ventura area in high school, and on a lucky summer day, just before school started, I went to the pool, and they both were there. We immediately hit it off and have been intertwined with each other's lives ever since.

Charley was the focused and driven one of the trio. She earned a master's degree and taught high school English. Whit was a bit of a wanderer but had found herself very successful in the hotel and restaurant business, mainly organizing significant, high-dollar events for corporations. They both had moved to the San Diego area, whereas I had stayed in Ventura to help my aunt and support my brother after his divorce.

We hashed out what Charley was going through. A new and quite jealous girlfriend of an old boyfriend, with whom Charley was still close friends, had decided to trash Charley and try to ruin her image by posting some information about her on a high school social page that was from years ago and really not even relevant. But Charley was a sensitive soul and desperately needed to be encouraged that all would be okay. So, we spent most of the day surrounding her with love and copious amounts of rosé. We had also offered plans to flatten the girls' tires or toilet paper her house, but Charley declined, saying she wanted to take the high road. I mean, I guess that's one way to do it—dear, gracious Charley.

So, I'm just a tiny bit tipsy, ok, maybe a lot tipsy, as I was waiting in line, looking at my phone, not paying any attention. I look up and step forward just as the man in front of me finishes and turns to walk away. I run straight into him - or I should say a wall of muscle that smells like a beach - with a slight hint of orange peel. My complete body slams against him, and I put my hands up to stop myself and feel his pecs. Nice, firm, well-formed pecs. I want to see them, I think, and I give a squeeze and realize what I've done immediately. With mortified eyes, I look up, and then words begin to come out of my mouth. I can't stop them.

"Oh god. I just grabbed your pecs. They are so nice. I've never felt pecs like that. Fuck. I'm so sorry." Hands to yourself, Mallory.

He responds to my apologies with "it's ok". I rasp out a barely audible "sorry". He pauses a moment, and he is saying words, but I don't hear any of them. He. Is. So. hot.

His hair is not long, but long enough to push back from his forehead in a very Superman way. He has a square jaw with just a slight 5 o'clock shadow, which makes me think he's usually a clean-shaven guy, but not a stern one. He has an almost sweet upturn to his mouth that looks playful and mischievous. And his mouth is perfect. Lips full and made for kissing and maybe more, and I can't stop staring at them. His eyes are almost a teal blue with dark eyebrows that make the blue stand out even more. It takes me mere seconds to register this. We do the thing where we can't decide which way to move to get out of the way; I go one way and he does the same a couple of times and then with a firm grip, he holds my shoulders and gently moves me to one side breaking my lip trance, steps to the other and says with a low, growl, "Enjoy your day." "I like your mouth." I blurt. God, what is wrong with me? I like your mouth. Who says shit like that? No one normal, that's for sure. I'm frozen and tongue-tied, and now I wish the floor would swallow me whole. I want to disappear, but I also want to get close to him again, smell him, feel that mouth on my skin. Gahh, he's leaving, and I recognize that voice. Why do I recognize that growly voice and those eyes? Jackson says I think I know everyone, but there is something familiar about this wall of a man. I take a deep breath to brush the thoughts away, but I secretly hope we run into each other again. He looks at me quizzically, placing his hand to his lips, "What…?"

"I…fuck…sorry. I just thought you had nice lips, and I really have no idea why I thought you'd like to know that, but sometimes words fly out of my mouth, and it's kind of a problem when I get nervous or excited." I gush.

He looks at me quizzically, and another flash of recognition crosses his face. "I...uh...I'm sorry. I just overheard you were going to the spa at the same time. Thought maybe we would cross paths again. You know, it's weird, I feel like I know you."

"Yeah, you shouldn't go around touching random strangers. I don't think we've met." I wink. "I think we will be on different sides of the spa. You know, men and women?" I gesture, pointing back and forth between us, smiling.

He apologizes again and turns to leave.

I continue with the concierge and confirm my massage. I picked the earliest one so I could have the whole day with my girls by the pool and head to the beach for a bit before I had to get into work mode. This event could be a huge boost for my business, and I need to be rested and focused. I decided then to move the trailer tomorrow. And suddenly, I have a glimmer of recognition and turn to call out and ask him if he's from Ventura, but I see him disappearing into the elevator. As luck would have it, I caught a glimpse of his butt. That was a nice butt.

No, Mallory. Down, girl. You are here to focus on your new business and your friends.

No men.

9 JAKE

I was able to score an ocean view room on the 3rd floor. It was one of their smaller rooms, but I didn't care. It was just me, and I tended to like a cozier room, anyway. I opened the mini bar and checked out the offerings: soda, water, Mango vodka seltzer (which I am allergic to), and Stella beers. I opt for a Stella and head to the shower. Nothing better than a shower beer. Now this is a vacation.

As I step into the hot water and let the months of stress roll down the drain, all I can think of is that girl. She put her hair up in a pile on top of her head; I'd like to let it out of that bun. As it falls around her shoulders, I imagine her stepping into the shower in her pink tank top, as the fabric wets her nipples, they harden and poke out, so perfect. Just begging to have my mouth on them. She comes to me, pressing herself against me and kissing my chest softly. I slide my hand up and down the length of my hardening cock as she kisses up my neck to my mouth. She slides down to her knees, taking my dick from my hand and sliding her tongue from the base, then around my balls and one long stroke up to the tip. She takes me into her mouth and slides me all the way to the back of her throat. I groan and begin to drive slowly into her mouth. I've never wanted to fuck a mouth more, and I pump harder as she sucks harder. She stands kissing me lightly on my lips and through the water dripping down her cheeks, whispers "please fuck me…" and then louder in a deeper voice "at the bar" and a loud thump. I'm shaken out of my fantasy just as I'm about to come. Wait. That wasn't her. What was that? Shit. I slap the wall of the shower and droop my shoulders.

"Jake, I'll meet you at the bar!" I hear Sam hollering from the bedroom and pound a single hard fist against my hotel room door. Shit. I was actually getting off to the thought of a girl I've seen for 30 seconds, and got interrupted! I think I've actually lost it. I've lost the mood, so I quickly shampoo my hair and wash off, finishing my shower quicker than I would have liked.

Heading into the bar, I see it's very crowded, and Sam is sitting by the window at a high top with a gorgeous redhead, AND a blonde. I'm meeting Marie for the first time, and from a visual standpoint, I can see why Sam likes her. She's tall - maybe 5'9" - and has quite the cleavage going on. He introduces us, and immediately, I think she's perfect for him. She is soft spoken and has a lovely southern lilt to her voice. "I'm just so thrilled to meet you, Jake. Sam speaks so highly of you. And how fortunate to have had such a long-term friend. I hope to get to know you better. And, this is my friend Amee. Sam sends me a look that clearly says, "Look what I got you?" I didn't know Marie was bringing a friend, and I shot Sam a look like, "What the actual fuck?" Not that I'm not interested in meeting women, and I'm sure Amee is great, but it's just that this one auburn-haired girl with the warm eyes and sweet little mouth will not stop haunting my thoughts.

"Sam, can I see you at the bar?" I say through my teeth. "Excuse us, we'll be back with drinks, ladies!"

"What the hell, Sam?" I groan, "You could have warned me!"

"I tried to, but you didn't answer the door. What were you doing in there?" He retorts.

"Showering," I say without looking at him.

"Ah, 'showering'. Of course." He chuckles, glancing toward my crotch.

"It's not like that," I lie, not even sounding believable to myself, "and stop looking at my crotch." I'm still thinking about the girl with auburn hair, warm brown skin, and perfect, pouty lips. Thinking about my filthy fantasy from the shower. "It's just that...there might be...uh...someone."

"Really?" He shouts, "I had no idea! Sorry man. I'll keep it casual."

I don't mention that this "someone" really isn't anyone at this point. But he doesn't need to know that -

yet. The bartender sets up our drinks, and we head back to the girls.

I resolve to keep it light, making sure I don't give Amee any ideas and joke, "Well, Marie, this guy is a catch. I'd snatch him up if my interests didn't lie elsewhere." She chuckles and says, "Lucky me," leaning in to give Sam a peck on the cheek. Amee's eyes light up, and I cringe slightly. What did I do?

We keep conversation light and fun. We talk about how we met and how my parents took Sam everywhere with us since I didn't have any siblings. We tell stories about our times as kids and the crazy things we did in high school. We laughed until tears rolled down our cheeks when I told them about the time Sam was in the high school play and his mom gave him flowers. He was in love with the lead and really wanted to get her flowers, but forgot. So, he gave her the flowers his mom had given him. The embarrassment happened when he realized he had forgotten to take the card his mom had written out of the flowers. The girl was very gracious, but he was mortified and couldn't look her in the eye for weeks. We call it the

Fucking Flower incident to this day. He did finally get over it, and they ended up dating for a while. Until he realized she was 'dating' a LOT of other guys at the same time.

After many stories and a couple more drinks, I check my watch and excuse myself. "Hey guys, I have an early massage tomorrow. I'm going to turn in and be a good boy." Marie smiled, and Amee looked slightly disappointed, but pulled out her phone and ordered a rideshare. I walk her out to the front of the hotel and apologize if she thought tonight was going to go differently, and tell her that I wasn't aware she was coming. She smiled sweetly and kissed me on the cheek. "I can see there is something already going on with you. Thanks for being up front with me. Whoever she is, she's lucky to have a guy so hooked on her. You are a nice guy. Good luck, Jake."

Was I that transparent? Jesus. I still hadn't even officially met this woman and couldn't stop thinking of her. I hoped after hearing that she was having a massage at the same time that they might cross paths in the spa, but I wasn't counting on it. The men and women go to different sides of the spa after checking in. But I wondered if they might see each other at the pool or waiting room. For now, I'll have to leave that and try to get some rest. But why do I lie down thinking about seeing her again and feel giddy like it's Christmas Eve? I'm fucked.

10 Mallory

I arrive at the spa at 8:15 as requested. I can't remember the last time I had such a great night's sleep. That super-luxurious bed, made by sweet, sweet sleep angels, plus the sound of the waves through the patio door we left open a couple of inches, was simply decadent and just what I needed going into such a stressful weekend ahead. I threw on one of the fluffy room robes over my bathing suit and slippers, left the girls sleeping soundly, and quietly closed the room door.

The plan for the day is: massage, brunch, and a fun snorkeling excursion with the girls, shower, and then see where the rest of the evening takes us. Today is all about my girls, and tomorrow will be prep for the event. This event will be a big day for Squeeze the Day and potentially a massive boost for the business. I even had to hire temporary employees to help with the workload. I hope to meet some other food truck vendors and get ideas and leads. I'm nervous but excited and shocked that I fell asleep as soon as my head hit the pillow.

The spa is situated in a little cottage detached from the main part of the hotel, just at the beginning of the sand on the beach. The lobby is bright but understated, soft instrumental music is playing, and the staff is sweet and soft-spoken, creating a very chill vibe. I'm so happy I decided to splurge a little on this, and I'm looking forward to having some much-needed downtime. After checking in, I get changed into the spa robe and sandals, and I head to the waiting area. The sound of ocean waves and soft music plays in the dimly lit room. A few other folks are waiting for services; each station has headphones, and they are all wearing them. I pour a cup of fruit-infused water, choose a chair away from the others, and put on the headphones. Getting comfortable, I smell something familiar. It's different than the lavender and eucalyptus that fills the room. It's a vague scent of orange peels, and the tingle begins to happen again between my legs. It smells like the man. THE man. From the lobby. I sit up straight to look, but I only see two blonde women chatting quietly and an older gentleman, perhaps in his 70s. No sign of the beautiful, kissable, blue-eyed man from the day before. Damn. I must be really hard up and imagining it. Relaxing back into my chair, I think, "But what if he were here?" I quickly wipe that thought from my mind. I don't have time or space for men right now. No men!

"Ms. Sweet," a soft female voice calls out. I sit up, excited and ready for this massage. At $250 an hour, this is a true splurge, and I don't want to miss a minute. I follow the girl dressed in her spa uniform, hair in a tight, sleek bun at the nape of her neck. As we exit toward the massage room, she turns and says with sorrowful eyes and a solemn expression, "My name is Jade. My apologies, Ms. Sweet. We have overbooked your time slot. As this is unacceptable, we can offer you a raincheck to return at a later date." This is so disappointing. NO! My beautiful massage is slipping away. "Alternatively," she continues, "We do also have a couples massage room where we can accommodate you." "YES!" I reply exuberantly. "…But, "she goes on, "You would have to share the space with the other client that we also overbooked, who has agreed to share the room.

Oh my. My eyes widen. I don't know. This situation seems odd. Can they actually do that? "How does that work?" I ask, "Who is it?" "I can't get naked in front of a strange man! It's a woman, right?"

She shoots a look at the waiting area and responds, looking at her clipboard, "Actually, I see a Mr. Reyes has agreed to share the room." Seeing the terror on my face, she continues, "It will all be very private for each one of you. You'll have your own therapist, and you won't even see each other or know each other is there unless you want to. I realize this is not ideal, and I'm happy to offer you a massage at a later date, but unfortunately, this is the best we can do today. We will also offer you a 50% discount."

"Fine," I say hesitantly, "but if this guy is a weirdo and tries to flash his junk at me, I'm holding you responsible for my trauma." She glances again at the waiting area and smiles awkwardly, "I assure you Mr. Reyes will not be flashing… his…er…junk at anyone."

11 Jake

I hear the girl, Jade, who informed me of the mix-up, speaking with a woman around the corner. I pause to listen, " …a Mr. Reyes has agreed to share the room." The woman then agrees as long as I don't 'flash my junk'?"

I head around the corner to defensively assure this woman I'm no flasher, "What kind of weirdo…" I freeze. The woman is standing there with Jade. THE woman. The auburn hair I thought about twisted in my hand, twisted on top of her head, her brown eyes looking straight into mine, making me look away, but not before I catch a glimpse of that sweet mouth. The one I fantasized about sucking me off in the shower. The one I imagined this morning as I woke up with my hand in my boxer briefs. Nope. Stop. I've got to pull it together.

Wait? She's the one sharing a massage room with me. My dick gets half hard with joy, and I have to keep looking at the ground to make sure it doesn't go full mast on me, and I become the aforementioned "creeper". Before I look down, her eyes go wide. "You?" she squeaks. Her cheeks turn pink, and I again imagine what it would be like to have her hands running all over my body, to kiss that bow mouth and have it all over my cock. The pictures in my head are filthy and hot, and I can't look at her yet. I keep my eyes diverted as long as possible.

"Um, yeah. It's me." I stutter. "We seem to keep running into each other. Awkwardly. I totally understand if you want to cancel your massage. I don't want to cramp your space."

"Me cancel?" she says incredulously. "Heck no. Maybe you need to cancel? I'm pretty sure I booked before you."

Jade interrupts, "Technically, yes, Ms. Sweet, you did. But we hoped since you were the last two to book that you would be willing to share."

"Ugh. So, I don't HAVE to share, but I have to be the dick if I don't want him with me?" she says,

"Listen," I say, hands up palms toward her in surrender, "It's fine. Take the room. I don't want you thinking I'm a weirdo." I can see she's wavering, so I decide to sweeten the offer. "Or, what if I pay? The whole cost of the room. No split, tip included. I'm really desperate for this massage, and I can see you are, too. So, let's share. We don't even have to know each other's names. Keep it anonymous." I say, instantly regretting it. Damn. Why did I suggest that? I want to know her. I want to meet her. Maybe spend a little time in my room with her. Nope, again. STOP. Am I becoming the weirdo she worried about? Fuck. I don't want to be a weirdo. I want to get to know her.

"Really? You'll pay, and there will be no contact during or after? No names?" She says, conceding, looking at me with suspicious eyes.

Thank fuck, I think. I REALLY need this massage. And I guess I'll have to believe that the universe has brought us together twice. It could happen again. Right? Sure, why not?

"Yes. No first names. Just massages and go our separate ways. Deal?" I place my hand out to shake.

She takes my hand, and I swear there is an electric current straight from my palm down my belly and into my cock. I growl, "Great." I'm sounding more in pain than resolved, and cough awkwardly to try to cover it up. She eyes me warily, "Mr. Reyes." She states. "Ms. Sweet," I respond as we turn to Jade.

"Lead the way." She says, "and just so you know, I'm not 'desperate' for anything."

"Noted." I follow, wondering what the fuck I've just gotten myself into.

A massage. Just a massage. And then we go on our way. Right? Right.

Jade opens the door to the massage room and lets her in, introducing her to her therapist, Liza, and mine,

Thelma. Liza is a late 30s-looking woman with a serene face and a sweet smile, her hair in a tight bun, and a confident grace.

Liza purrs, "Ms. Sweet, please go ahead and get comfortable under the sheet, face down, and I'll be with you shortly. You may take off everything or only what you are comfortable with. Please remove any jewelry and place it in the envelope on the table."

Thelma is a bit older, maybe 50, and very possibly was a powerlifter in another life. She looks very uh, strong and has a serious, no-nonsense look on her face. Did they do this on purpose? Are they trying to scare me into not being a weirdo? *Ok, Thelma, I see you.* I think.

Thelma says with just a slight German accent and a stern tone, "Wait here. I'll get you when she is ready. No peeky."

"Of course, no 'peeky'," I scoff. What the hell? Why does everyone think I'm a Peeping Tom weirdo? Geez.

When I enter the room, she is already in there, settled on her table. The light is turned low, and soft music with nature sounds is playing. I try to keep my eyes diverted, I really do, but fuck if I don't glance up to see she is already uncovered from the waist up. Her therapist begins rubbing her hands with oil. I can't see much, but I do see her hair brushed to one side. It's long and sleek and begging for my fingers to run through it. Damnit. I AM a peaky weirdo. I quickly look away and try to get settled. I can't decide whether to remove my boxer briefs. I usually would, but now everyone has me terrified that I'm a pervert trying to catch a glimpse of a stranger naked, and I don't want Thelma to headlock me, thinking I'm trying to flash Ms. Sweet. Also, it might be better to add an extra layer of protection, just in case there's accidental evidence of said peeking. That I absolutely will not be doing!

As I start to relax, Thelma enters. She uncovers my back, and holy shit, Thelma is strong. She begins to knead and rub my shoulders. It's not painful or too much, but this girl can REALLY dig in. I'm actually grateful for this woman because I have had massages before that left me feeling less than satisfied. I have a feeling Thelma is going to get a BIG tip. I settle in and try to be in the moment, as they say.

I hear rustling from the other side of the room and then a long moan. "Oh, that's it. Right there." She says, moaning in pleasure.

And I'm dead. I don't know if I can do this. If I were on my back, those added layers might not make a difference. Hearing this hot girl make those noises is not helping me stay in my lane. Not one bit.

Again, she instructs Liza, "Oh yes. Deeper and a little harder, please." She requests. "Of course, ma'am. Please let me know if this feels ok." Liza whispers.

I feel blood rush to my dick, making it half hard, and try not to squirm, imagining myself doing things to make her make those sounds, and with my name attached. I definitely shouldn't be imagining that AT ALL, and I must pull myself together. Then the room goes quiet. Ok. If she doesn't do THAT, I think I can make it. But so far, this is not relaxing. All I can think about is her lying a few feet away, naked and moaning things I wouldn't mind hearing in my bed. I try to focus on the music and listing condiments to make my libido go down - mustard, ketchup, salt, pepper, whipped cream…mmm…licking whipped cream…NOoooo…soy sauce, vinegar, wasabi…and as my list dwindles, she finally seems to quiet, and my own massage takes over. No more pervy stranger thoughts. Just peaceful relaxation.

12 Mallory

As Liza finishes with what may have been the best massage of my life by dragging her fingers through my hair, I take a deep breath.

"Ms. Sweet," Liza says softly, "please take your time getting up, please enjoy the water left on the counter, drink plenty throughout the day, and I'll meet you outside whenever you are ready."

"Thank you so much," I whisper.

I'm so thankful that I didn't give up my spot, and really, after the first few minutes, I didn't even realise Mr.

Reyes was in there. I'm not really sure He paid any attention either. It did take me a minute to erase the thoughts of this sexy, gruff man naked under a sheet a mere 4 feet away, but I was able to block out the noise and enjoy my moment.

And then, the loudest, most obnoxious snore breaks through my Zen moment. I startle and snap my head to look at him. He slightly opens his eyes, eyelashes fluttering confusedly. Thelma slaps her hand over her mouth and tries not to laugh. She looks at me and then puts a finger to her lips, indicating to be very quiet for our sleeping beauty, and runs her hands through his hair one more time to help him go back to sleep. I can't help but smile looking at his large frame draped in a sheet. He looks so relaxed and peaceful. He seems to have needed this. I'm glad we shared after all.

Thelma is finishing his massage with her fingers in his hair. I'm staring too long, and I have a half a second where I imagine dragging my fingers through that gorgeous dark, wavy hair, then pushing off the sheet to reveal what is clearly a solid and ripped body all the way down to see what he's got between his legs, and my nipples are now at attention. Ack. What am I thinking! That's inappropriate, and I need to get the hell out of here before he wakes up. I'm starting to be the creeper. This is not a thing that can happen. I don't hook up with strangers.

I look back to Liza waiting for me at the door, returning the finger to my lips to "shhhh", hastily donning my robe, grabbing my slippers, taking one last look at the beautiful man sleeping peacefully and tiptoeing out. It takes everything I have not to look back one more time for a final glimpse at this hot man. But I restrain myself and quietly close the door.

I head back to sit by the spa pool and have a light lunch before going to get ready for my afternoon with the girls. We've planned a meet-up at a snorkelling place in La Jolla, and then have dinner at a rooftop spot. We are soaking up the few hours before we actually have to work and get Charley back in a somewhat happy place.

The afternoon is glorious. The sky is clear and fresh. The water was clear too, so we were able to see so many fish and sea stars. I love the bright Garibaldi, and the sea lions were extra playful, keeping us entertained for hours. When we finally dragged ourselves off the beach, sun toasted and sandy, and called the rideshare back to the hotel, we were tired in such a good way. Our cheeks were pink, and our muscles felt spent and ready for a hot shower and a cocktail.

When we returned to the hotel, we decided to stop by the bar on our way up to the room and grab a drink to take up to the room.

The bar was filled with people in business attire who looked like they were at a networking event. Women in tight but professional skirt suits and men in sharply pressed shirts and ties chatted and sipped cocktails. We clearly stood out in our rumpled beach attire and seawater hairstyles, but we thought it was funny, so we just headed in as we belonged.

As we waited for our drinks, a low, gruff, but somewhat familiar voice behind me growled, "Can I get those drinks for you, Ms. Sweet?" I didn't turn, but Charley and Whitney did and then looked at me with stunned expressions. I felt his voice more than heard it; it was a low rumble close to my ear. "I hope your massage was deep and relaxing enough this morning. I didn't get to say goodbye." I felt a warmth and tingle between my thighs, and if I hadn't been a touch sunburnt on my cheeks, it would have been undeniable that my body was responding to his words.

"You all look like you've had a fun day. What did you get up to? Can I buy your drinks?" He asked. My voice came out as a squeak at first, and I cleared my throat to try again, "I think…I think we've passed the 'can I buy you a drink' phase, don't you, Mr. Reyes?" turning to him with a bit of a sultry look. I should not encourage this man, but I also cannot resist the banter. He looked so good in his fitted button-up shirt, worn untucked, with jeans and some Vans tennis shoes. Put together enough to show he cares, but also casual and sexy. But I don't know anything about him, where he lives or why he is here. He could be on his honeymoon or on a family vacation. That would make the couple's massage this morning even more awkward, but hey, who am I to judge? I could judge a newly married man having a massage with another woman in the room. But I'm NOT looking for a relationship, so it doesn't matter.

Charley eyeballs me, squinting, "Do you KNOW this man?" What is going on here?"

I scoff, still not turning around to give him any attention, "I don't know him. We met briefly this morning. That is all. We should go."

Mr. Reyes has clearly had a couple of drinks and is feeling playful. "Oh, come on now, Ms. Sweet, have you already forgotten our massage this morning?" He drawled playfully.

"But what's he talking about? Massage?" she whispers, "Did you hook up and not tell us?"

I hadn't mentioned this morning to the girls, no talk of the massage or this gorgeous creature that keeps popping up on this trip. I didn't feel it was necessary or needed any energy, since nothing was going to come of it. But I was starting to wonder. This was the third time in only hours we had crossed paths, and it was getting harder to ignore the attraction that was building. Was that attraction, or was it lust? It had been so long that I wasn't entirely sure. What I was sure about was that his voice did things to my lady parts. Were my nipples hard because of the cool breeze or his breath near my shoulder? I'm thinking the latter.

He noticed the questioning look in Whitney's eyes, and his eyes grew wide "OHHHHH, you haven't told your friends." He laughed.

"Well, I'm not surprised," he chuckles, "when I woke up after the massage, snoring and drooling, I guessed that you made a quick getaway and never spoke of it. I was really hoping to say thank you for sharing with me."

"Sharing? Massage? What the fuck, Mal…" Charley starts to say, and I clap a hand to her mouth.

Mr. Reyes sucks in a breath, eyes wide and lets it out, "Well, damn. I almost had your first name."

I shake my head, indicating that we are not sharing names. "Yes, it was an amazing massage. And thank you again for paying. That was more than generous."

"It was the least I could do, since you agreed to share the room. And you can be assured I didn't peek at all. No peeky weirdo!" He smiles broadly, winking.

The look in his eyes tells me he has more to say. Much more. And I pause because I think I want to hear more. My interest is piqued. He is funny, charming, and oh-so-hot, and I want to know more. I can listen to Aunt Mel in my head telling me to give him a shot, so I decide that I'm going to take some initiative to see if he wants to meet up later after dinner. Just then, a blonde with tits to her chin, dressed in a suit that looks like someone sewed it on her body, walks over and places a hand on his shoulder, and eyes me up and down, "We have that sit down with the Clardy Group right now. You good?"

I look back and forth from him to her and realise the mistake I have made. Although it's apparent they have a business relationship, there might be more. I'm not here to become part of a triangle. So, I don't say anything.

He looks disappointed that she has interrupted us, but turns to us and smiles, with a dear-God-what-the-actual-fuck panty melting smile that I may never recover from, "Unfortunately, ladies, I must attend to some business. Hopefully, we will meet again, and I can get your first name. Until then." He raises his glass and steps back.

At that moment, the bartender drops our drinks at the bar, and I turn to him and hold up my glass as a toast and call to him as he walks away, "Here's to possible chance meetings with strangers. Mr. Reyes." He turns, and his eyes lock on mine for just a moment, and I see a darkening, or was that my imagination again? He strides back to me, leans close, lifting his eyebrows and says, "We are hardly strangers at this point, remember?" He takes my hand and kisses it lightly on the back, his lips lingering just a little too long. And had I been wearing panties, they would have been officially gone. Poof. Melted. Gah! Who is this man, and why does he keep popping up in my day? And I, too, can't shake that little feeling of disappointment low in my belly. And where the hell is that coming from? I think I just had a mini orgasm. Is that a thing? I think I just made it a thing. Lord, I really need to get laid, or maybe just some time with my little friend in my toiletry bag.

The girls grab their drinks and me by the arm, "Let's go. You've got some explaining to do." They announce as we head to the elevator. Whitney turns and wiggles her fingers at him and says, "Goodbye, Mr. Mysterious massage man."

I postponed my confession when we entered the room and saw the merciful message light blinking. I quickly headed to the phone, "Ohhhh gotta check the message!" I chirped, laughing. The girls groaned.

The message was from the spa saying I had left my credit card after purchasing some of their decadent body wash and rushing out. I hung up and let the girls know that I wanted the first shower as I needed to run down to retrieve it before they closed for the night. Whitney insisted that if they didn't hear the whole story at dinner, I would be locked in the room and unable to go to my work event tomorrow. "Ok, ok," I said, "there is nothing to tell, but I will tell you about it, which is literally nothing. Less than nothing."

Charley called out from the bathroom, "Ohhhh, ok. Is that why that freaking gorgeous man was trying to buy our drinks and whispering at your neck like he wanted to eat you? You're not getting off that easy. You WILL tell us."

I laughed, ran in to take a quick shower, threw on a pair of shorts and a tank top, and grabbed my flip-flops. Running out, I let the door slam to punctuate and postpone telling these gossip-hungry hens the story that really wasn't even a story. Yet.

But it was true. My mystery man had seemed very interested in me. But why? And what was the story with the blonde? I wouldn't be mad if we met again, but that was unlikely. I surely wouldn't run into him again in the next couple of days. I just needed to keep my head down, get through the event and head back to my safe little town.

13 Jake

I sit around the table with four executives from a very prestigious real estate group, my personal assistant Bethany, who, thank the gods, is taking copious notes, and Blake Shaver, the general manager of two of my more successful restaurants– the one in Laguna near where I live and the one in San Diego. I know they are talking about essential things about my business, but I cannot focus.

All I can think of right now is her- M? What did she say? May, Mar, Mal? Sweet. She is, without question, the most gorgeous woman I've ever seen. Each time I see her, I become more enamored. She carries herself with such confidence and grace. Today, she looked fresh from the beach. Her cheeks and shoulders were slightly pink, most likely from a little too much sun. She twisted her hair into a messy knot at the back of her neck, and she had a tiny heart tattoo that, when he had gotten close enough at the bar, I could see it said "Dianne" scripted into the side. Her legs extended from a yellow sundress that was just a little too fucking short, just to see a little bit of cheek at the top of her leg. And yes, damn it, I'd tried not to look, but fuck me if I hadn't glanced just a second. I mean, I have eyes in my head. And that only served to make me half hard with nothing to do about it but think about her without the dress in my hotel room....no, no no. But I want to know her first name. I want to learn more about her. Is she with anyone? She seems way out of my league. Everyone is wondering how much I've been working lately. "...Mr. Reyes?....JAKE?" A loud voice broke him out of his fantasy. Bethany was tapping his arm.

"Oh shit," I mumbled "I'm so sorry. Just a lot on my mind. Please go on, sir."

Mr. Ellis smirked uncomfortably, "I was just mentioning that we need some fresh ideas to open a new location in the area. We feel the beachy, dive bar vibe is getting a little played out. We need something fresh and more....er...fun." He said the word like it tasted awful, and he needed to spit it out as quickly as possible.

"Fun," I mused, albeit a bit irritated. "Well, we will have to mull that over. We have set up most of our restaurants for different kinds of fun. But, please, if you have suggestions, I'm all ears. Now, if that's it, we all have a long day tomorrow, and I'd like to get some rest." I hated meetings like these with executives who had no idea what it was actually like to run a restaurant. All five of my locations were very successful, and it fucking pissed me off that this real estate guy thought they needed more "fun".

They all offered their pleasantries and went their separate ways.

Bethany shut down her notebook and slid it into her bag. "I'm going to grab a glass of wine and sink into a bubble bath in that glorious room you got me."

I held her at her elbow and looked at her sincerely, "Thanks for all you do. Maybe we can meet a little early tomorrow to go over the notes you got tonight and come up with a game plan for the event tomorrow based on what these guys are looking for?" I responded.

There was a flicker in her eyes, and she smiled seductively but he brushed it away "I can go over it tonight if you like? It won't take long. That way, you can give it some thought before tomorrow."

I didn't really want to hang out with her. I knew she had harbored a bit of a crush, and I had tried to let her know gently that I wasn't interested, so this might be a bad idea, but I did need to get this going in my head. Reluctantly, I agreed, "Ok. Come on up to my room after you get your wine. We can sit on the balcony and chat about it for a while." I paid my tab, swallowed the last sip of my gin and soda and headed to the elevator.

I saw Bethany chatting with the hostess at the restaurant and assumed she'd take a while getting her drink, so I could change and have a minute to myself. Just a few steps away from the elevator, I saw it closing and going up. "Hold the door, please," I called. The doors opened; I stepped in, looking down, and mumbled a "thanks." A slightly familiar voice laughed softly "This can't be fucking for real."

I catch the scent of lavender and turn slowly to see her lovely pink cheeks and hair draped around her shoulders, wet and freshly washed, wearing shorts and a string tank top, "Ms. Sweet. We DO have to stop meeting like this." I say, as I imagine pushing her to the back wall of the elevator and smashing my lips against hers until we both can't breathe. She's already backed against it. It wouldn't take much to turn, hold her hands in place above her head, and make her mine, tasting her lips and inhaling her amazing scent. God, what the hell am I thinking? I don't even know her, but we keep meeting. There must be something to this? She breathed out a petite pant and whispered, "You look like you…need…something. Mr. Reyes. Is everything ok?" His heart was beating so fast, he loved to hear her say his name like that, and he thought maybe she could sense it. I do need something. I need my hands on your tits and my head between your legs, and you to come on my face. But I don't say that because what the fuck? But yeah, I definitely need something.

"I uh…was just…er…thinking…would you want to come on my balcony. Shit, what am I saying? No, come over to sit on my balcony and hear the water. Um, the ocean, not like the water in the room." He babbled. Damn I'm fucking this up. The elevator door dinged and opened.

"This is me." She said, smiling, "While I would most likely very much enjoy coming on your balcony and hearing water, I have my friends waiting for me. Have a good night." She brushed her hand across his shoulder, wiggled her fingers in a wave, and stepped out just before the door closed.

14 Mallory

After two bottles of champagne, the most amazing dinner I've had in months, and laughing until we almost peed-actually, Charley did a few times, which made us laugh even harder - and me finally coming clean about the last 36 hours and my multiple meetings with Mr. Reyes, we were well and truly drunk. And even though I had to work tomorrow, I was so glad I had come to hang out with my girls. We never grew tired of being together after 15 years of friendship; these were truly the times I held dear. There were no secrets between us. We had been through thick and thin; even a few years passed when life got in the way. They both moved to San Diego, and we didn't talk.

None of us remembers why, but eventually Whitney reconnected us all as we had never missed a beat. I couldn't live without the love and support of these girls.

"I cannot lie to you girls. This man is so smoking hot, and we keep ending up in the same place. But it's just a coincidence. There isn't any meaning to it. I do want to pursue it, but he lives in Laguna. It's dumb. Never mind." I say matter-of-factly, like I'm mainly trying to convince myself.

"Do you think there is something to it?" Charley asks. "It seems like a LOT of chance meetings. If I were you, I would be on his balcony right NOW and finding out for sure. That man is suspiciously hot."

Whitney, ever the pragmatic, chimes in, "If it's truly meant to be, you'll see him again. The universe is just being a tease right now. I mean, I'm not saying you shouldn't have jumped on that meat train, but I'm certain if it's a thing, you'll cross paths soon."

"My god, Whitney. Please don't call it a meat train. That sounds like a name for a deli sandwich. I know you're not into dick, but don't ruin it for the rest of us who love it." I laugh. "Ok. I'm glad I didn't go because I wanted to have this time with you. I miss you guys, and I think I'm going to be getting busier with the lemonade stand if tomorrow goes well. And Aunt Mel keeps me busy, too; she's been so lost since Mom passed. Honestly, I'm a little nervous about leaving her if I have events with the stand."

Charley nodded, "I totally get your anxiety. But you have always made things happen. I know you are going to pull this off. And you have Jackson to help with your aunt. And you know that we are just a couple of hours away. We can be there to pick up any slack if you need us."

Whitney sighs, "What would you do without us? I mean, who else would swoop in and get you drunk and tell you to wait to fuck the hottest man to hit on you in a very long time? We are your true friends."

We're all laughing now because, honestly, what the fuck? I could have had a gorgeous man between my legs tonight, but I chose these crazy girls! I do love them, but now I'm feeling very cockblocked.

Charley had been talked off her ledge, which was the main reason we had this meet-up, and we assured her that this chick, who was trying to sabotage her, didn't have a leg to stand on, and if she did, we'd sweep it Karate Kid style and take her down. She needed to get back home tomorrow to make lesson plans and prep for her classes on Monday, so she went to bed. Whitney had met a cute girl in the bar, and they had made plans to meet up for an early breakfast, so she was heading to get some sleep, too. I had done all my prep for the job tomorrow and wasn't feeling quite ready to sleep. I decided to turn the lights down so the girls could get some sleep and head out to the balcony to listen to the water by myself. I slipped out quietly, laughing to myself about my encounter with Mr. Reyes in the elevator.

I'm trying to maintain indifference. I'm not in a place to be in a relationship. I just started a new business; I live with my brother and help take care of my aunt, who has had two bouts with cancer and is currently in remission. While she fully supports my independence and would never advocate for me putting my love life on hold, she does need me. Since my mom, her sister, and best friend

115

died 3 years ago, she has no one else to depend on entirely. She has an ex-husband who lives in Minnesota, and they don't talk anymore. They never had kids together, so Jackson and I are her "kids". It just doesn't feel right to attempt a serious relationship, or really anything that would take time away from her. I need to focus on being there for her and running my business. I know if I ask her, she would definitely say, "Mal, my girl, we need to squeeze everything out of life as long as you've got breath in you to breathe. You don't want to let anything pass you by. Long after I'm gone, you'll thank me. Go fuck a hottie for me!" Easier said than done, Auntie.

Except that I can't stop thinking about Mr. Reyes. The many-degrees-hotter-than-the-sun man that I keep running into.

I sat with my feet up on the railing and sipped sparkling water, listening to the waves crash below. There really is nothing better than the sound of the ocean. I was chuckling, recounting him asking me to "come on his balcony". Wondering if I should have taken him up on it. I don't really do one-night stands, but maybe there could be something more to it? The resort isn't huge, but it's weird to run into him multiple times and share a massage room with him. So, we've technically already been naked in the same room. And there go my lady parts again. I'm thinking of him and how good he smelled and how sexy his butt looked in his jeans. Sigh.

The night was quiet, and only a few lights twinkled in the distance. I took a deep breath of the salty ocean air and reveled in the beautiful space and time. Tomorrow was going to be a busy day. I ran through the operation in my head. I had arranged for a large rental freezer on hand to house my frozen cocktails and hired a couple of young servers to serve throughout the day. I set up my pay-point in case of extra orders. And as I ran through my timeline in my head, I heard a giggle and a whispered and somewhat drunk-sounding, "I promise I won't tell anyone in the office."

And then an increasingly familiar gruff voice, "Come on, let's get you to bed."

I inhale sharply and freeze, my heart rate quickening. What in the actual fuck? No. Really? It couldn't be. It was hard to make out the voices, but that was definitely a familiar one. Well, isn't that just a kick to the gut? It seems Mr. Reyes has other interests lined up. Wow. As soon as I said no to coming to his room, he had already found someone else. Apparently, he's got an office fling going. Well, if one thing is for sure, I dodged a bullet there. I'm not interested in being on a list of someone's playthings. Now I understand the flirtatiousness, and I'm realizing it's just as well. I don't need any romantic entanglements anyway, and I would likely have never seen him again. But why did he have to be right above me? Is this the universe taunting me with the promise of something good, then ripping it from me, or protecting me from the inevitable? Just another fucking guy with his words that lure you in and make you think things could go your way with love. Only to have my heart smashed again. I'm just not falling for it.

I slip back inside my room and head to the bathroom to brush my teeth.

Lying down in the bed, I am so comfortable in my satin pajamas and cozy comforter, but I don't feel comfy at all.

I feel something that doesn't make sense, and the anticipation of adventure is gone. I feel like I lost something that I never even had. I don't even know the man's first name, for God's sake!

I feel sad. For what might have been. Not just with the mystery man but with Adam. As a tear runs down my face, I chastise myself for such naivety, wondering if I'll ever get it right, and I close my eyes and drift to sleep.

15 Jake

Before Bethany arrived, I changed out of my suit pants, shirt, and tie into some comfortable sweats and a t-shirt, just as there was a knock on the door. I opened the door to find her with a bottle of champagne on ice and two glasses. "I wasn't sure if you wanted a drink, so I just got this. Do you like Champagne, Jake?" She said just a little too casually, running her long red fingernail down my chest to right above my waistband. She was definitely not in business mode. She hooked her heels on her finger, and her top was unbuttoned just one too many for my liking. Don't get me wrong, Bethany is lovely, but I do not mix business with pleasure, or dating AT ALL. This is a hard-and-fast rule for me. I can't juggle the complications it promises, especially with someone who works directly for me. So, when I see all that is going on with Bethany at my door looking more like she wants to have a special meeting with my cock, I think Oh no no no. This is not what is happening here. "I'm good. I don't want to drink anything else tonight. I don't want to be groggy in the morning." I told her, maybe a little more gruffly than I needed to.

"Ok, no problem. It's here if you change your mind." She trilled and dropped her heels by the door, and I cringed. I really hoped she didn't think this was more than it was. I had done everything I could since I hired her to keep things very professional. She looked as if she were making herself very comfortable.

We headed to the balcony, and she poured herself a glass of champagne.

"Jaaaakey," she drawled. Her Georgia upbringing came out when she had a few drinks, he noticed at a few after-work happy hour events.

"Let's get to the rundown for tomorrow." I put on my 'all business' voice and hoped she would get the hint. The event tomorrow was a super-networking event. All kinds of bar and restaurant owners, managers, chefs, suppliers, and real estate folks from the area would be meeting. Chefs would be cooking small bites, bartenders making cocktail sips, which are tastes of new cocktails and non-alcoholic offerings that were getting very popular in many spaces. There would be a few food truck offerings. The company had invited a handful of tried-and-true food trucks as a treat for everyone who attended, and then added a few new truck vendors to help them connect with other restaurants and bars to gather ideas or find chefs who needed a place to work. Owners could get fresh ideas to try at their locations to boost business, and realtors could find possible new restaurants for buildings that had recently become vacant or new builds looking for a hot, fresh spot for a neighborhood. Jake had run this event in a couple of other areas, and it had always been very lucrative for most people involved. This was the second San Diego area event, and it had grown. They managed to get a space near the fairgrounds, which had worked out great since Sam and I had Ivy Jane's concert to attend.

She plopped into one of the patio chairs and pulled out her computer with a pouty look on her face. "Fine," she began running down everything. "Here is the list of vendors, chefs, and food trucks. We will position them according to this chart to ensure maximum accessibility for everyone. I marked the check-in spot with a star, and everyone will have a lanyard that clearly shows their preferred name and the category they are participating in. Everyone will be allowed a sample of each food and drink, and vendors may sell additional items beyond one drink or food item if they choose. Everyone is also allowed to exchange information, but no meetings or making of meetings should happen at the event since we have a finite amount of time at the venue, and we want everyone to have an equal chance."

She let out a long breath, "Does that all sound ok?" I tried to contain my somewhat shocked expression. I knew Bethany was a hard worker and did a lot behind the scenes, but this was over and above. She had really gotten this organized down to the tiny details. I was starting to feel a little guilty and like a royal dickhead for blowing her off. I really don't have any romantic feelings for her, but I figured, why not have one glass of champagne to toast the event and say thank you for a job well done. It felt like it was getting into a little bit of a gray area, but I could stop it if it went too far.

"Bethany, this is fantastic. You have done an excellent job on this event, and I'm so grateful. Why don't you go ahead and pour me a glass, and we can toast to your success?" I said enthusiastically.

Her smile was shy at first. "Really?" She said in a small voice, and then the smile overtook her whole face, as though it was the first time anyone had celebrated her success. I realized at this point I needed to make sure to encourage my employees more. I have curated a stellar team and need to let them know I appreciate them.

We held up our glasses, and I toasted. "Cheers to Bethany and the future of Driftwood! And thank you for all of your hard work!" We clinked and sipped. Well, I sipped, and she downed half the glass. Ok. Well, that's one way to do it.

"Thank you, Mr. Reyes. It means a lot. I did put a lot of effort into making this a success. I love planning events like this! But you made it possible for me to really make it special for everyone coming. And for me to stay in such a cool spot. This resort is so beautiful, and I really want to thank you. You have made this job so much better than I ever thought it would be." She gushed.

And before I could even react, she was leaning into me, grabbing a handful of my shirt front, and pulling my mouth to hers. I freeze for a second, my brain taking its sweet time figuring out how to react. "Bethany!" I held her firmly at her shoulders, pushing her back, trying not to be rough or embarrass her, and then stood us up together. She reluctantly released my shirt. "We cannot do this. You know that, right? You are an amazing woman and co-worker, but I cannot be involved with an employee. Especially not my PA. I thought you understood this?" I barked, perhaps sounding a little angrier than I meant to.

But I really needed to drive home the point. I don't want to lose her as my PA, and it just wouldn't work.

She laughed nervously, obviously pink-cheeked and embarrassed, but not totally swayed from trying, "Are you suuuure? I promise I won't tell anyone in the office." She drawled a little too loudly, sounding VERY southern now. The alcohol surely emboldens her, and she needs to sleep it off, I think.

I soften my tone and hold her up, "Let's get you to bed."

She makes a pouty face. "Your bed?"

I growl, and she pouts again but concedes.

"Ok. I get it." She whispers and heads to the door.

She is only a few rooms down from mine, so I walk her to her room and make sure she is safely inside, telling her to lock the deadbolt. I set her phone alarm for 7:30 just in case the champagne makes her forget, and tell her I'll see her in the lobby at 9 am.

As I get back to my room, I take off my t-shirt and sweats and climb into bed. While I'm plugging in my phone, it dings with a text.

Bethany: I'm sorry, boss.

Me: You're fine. Get some rest. We have a long day tomorrow.

As I drift to sleep, I only have thoughts of Ms. Sweet. I really hope I get another chance with her.

16 Mallory

I actually slept better than I thought I would. However, I did have a very bizarre dream that I wanted to dress like Madonna for the event. My dad was wearing the white frilly socks I needed to complete my outfit, and he would not hand them over. This is what stress does to me, my friends.

I looked at my phone for a few minutes, perusing the event schedule for today. Check-in and setup start at 10, and the realtors and other guests arrive at 12. The event seems very well planned. They have held it two years in a row, and this is my first one. I'm very excited to meet other food truck owners, chefs, and people in the business. I need to network. I'm very new in the industry, and haven't done much to get my name out there. I have been playing it safe and have only done a couple of small local events. I'm ready to dip my toe in with the big dogs. A very successful restaurateur also runs the event. I'm really hoping to meet him at least.

Whitney already left for her breakfast date, and I've got the room to myself. I needed this space to work out what I'm feeling before I go put on my game face for work. I can't help thinking about what I heard from the balcony above me, and I finally decide that it was a stroke of luck to listen to that. Now I know that, even if I ever saw him again, he's not the type of guy I would want. Any man who takes advantage of a co-worker is not worth the breath they breathe.

I don't blame her one bit; he is so sexy. Damn, those eyes and that perfectly tousled hair and his scent of oranges and leather. I bet he had a little hair on his chest, which was probably beautiful and chiseled, judging by the tiny little squeeze I gave it the first time I saw him. I know it would be lovely to run my fingers through it. Shit, I was starting to get turned on by thinking about him again, and it needed to stop. Ok, right after my shower, I'm going to erase him from my brain—just one thing to do first.

I dug around in my travel bag and shamelessly took my favorite travel vibrator to the shower. Mr. Reyes, I think you owe me this fantasy. And I absolutely thought of him and what he might do on his knees with his head between my legs and his mouth covering my pussy, with the help of my little friend, making my inner walls pulse and clench as I came, saying his name. Thinking this might make me forget him was a fool's game, I now realize, but it was worth the effort.

Feeling sated and refreshed from my shower, I finished getting ready. I chose dark blue jeans and a tank top with lemons on it, which I had printed with "Squeeze the Day!" I bought matching lemon shirts for the servers, too, to make it look like a uniform. I was starting to get excited and ready to share my creation. So many hours of preparation and hard work had gone into this day. I really hoped that this would be a turning point for my business.

As I arrived at the venue, many folks were already getting set up, and the decorations were beautiful. We were on the fairgrounds in one of the hangars, which was decorated to look like a fun restaurant with tables, chairs, fire pits, and lights strung everywhere. There was even a dance floor. It was simple, yet it made for just the right ambiance. The food trucks were stationed at the open end of the building, and the rest of the booths and tables were just inside. They had a makeshift bar area that was about 16 feet long, and each bartender had their own setup of liquors and mixers they would be making. There were eight food trucks in total. Mine was definitely the smallest and most niche, which made me so happy. The potential of this event was limitless, and being 1 of 8 trucks at a high-end networking event could be a significant boost to my business. My adrenaline was racing.

Lively music was playing, and the space was filling up fast. The place smelled of good food, had a fun atmosphere, and a few people were even dancing. I had told my servers to be playful and really engage with the patrons. These were not just people out to have a drink and a good time. I really needed these folks to love what I had created. I know it's not for everyone, but it will be for someone. We served our special frozen drinks to so many people, and the reception was terrific. Everyone seemed intrigued by the concept.

"Hi, what would you like to try?" I called out to a guy standing and looking at the options.

"This is a really cool thing you have. What a unique idea. I'll take whatever you recommend." He says.

I pull out my personal favorite. "This is the lavender lemonade. This one is an homage to my hometown."

He takes it and takes a sip from the straw. "Oh, this is so good! Very nice! Where's your hometown?"

"It's up near Santa Barbara, a little town in the valley called Ojai." I smile.

"Oh, of course! We know Ojai well. My name is Sam. My buddy owns the Driftwood in Ventura. Do you know

Jake? He's the one who put this event on." He holds out his hand to shake mine.

"Oh my gosh! I live in Ventura, and Driftwood is our absolute favorite. Nice to meet you, Sam. Yes, I knew it was his event, but I haven't met him in person yet. I'm just so honored to be invited. It has been an amazing day." I say excitedly.

"I'm sure he would love to meet you. If you are going to be here hanging out, I'll go grab him." He says.

I point to the line forming, "I'm not going anywhere, but here's my card just in case." Handing him my business card, a magnet shaped like a lemon.

A line has been forming, and the servers are struggling a bit to keep up, so I jump back in to help. We have almost caught up, and as we are chatting with the last couple of people waiting, I look up and see Sam and the person with him. I assume this is the "buddy" Jake. But, I'm frozen. What is going on? Is the universe playing a joke on us? He cannot be the same person. The man who is walking towards my stand is not just some guy. No, this isn't a random businessman friend of a friend.

It's Mr. Reyes.

17 Jake

I'm looking across the hangar at the food truck area where Sam is taking me to meet a woman from Ventura who apparently loves Driftwood. A woman with an Airstream trailer transformed it into a mobile lemonade stand. What the fuck is going on this week?

As we walk towards the open door, three people stop me to introduce me to other local restaurant managers and owners, and then I see the trailer. It's familiar, yet it's painted a bright sunny yellow with lemons on it. Why do I feel a weird sense of déjà vu? My brain is trying to compute. I have met the same woman multiple times in awkward situations. I am now seeing a trailer and, in my head, I'm hearing a woman rambling and describing her dream of having a lemonade stand. Is this real life?

I see the shape of a woman in the trailer's window. I can't make out her face clearly, but it's familiar and so out of context. My brain is trying to calculate what is going on. Is this something from a dream I had? Is Sam trying to punk me?

I hear Sam rambling about the trailer-"it's an adult lemonade stand"-and the woman said she doesn't know me, and oh yeah, here's her card. I take the card, but cannot pull my eyes from the woman in the window. As I get closer, I see her eyes widen, and a look of panic crosses her face. I stop, dumbfounded. Ms. Sweet? I look at Sam, who has stopped a few steps ahead of me and is beckoning me. "Dude," he calls, "what are you doing? Are you ok?"

"Yeah…I…um…" I croak out to him, but I don't think he can hear me. My heart is racing, and I feel my dick pulse just the slightest bit, making my suit pants tighten. How is this happening? I look down at the card. It's a magnet shaped like a lemon. 'Squeeze the Day – a

136

Mobile Adult Lemonade Stand' owner/operator, Mallory Sweet, Ventura, CA. I stare at the card, and my feet won't move. I am in utter confusion. I feel Sam's hand on my shoulder. "Man, you look like you've seen a ghost. What's up?"

"This is her, Sam. The girl from the resort. You know, when I said I thought I might have met someone?" I say quietly, "I really thought I had missed the opportunity, but now she's here, and fuck, it's freaking me out. This is the 5th time in 3 days that I have run into her. And to clinch it all, that's the trailer - our trailer that I sold last year. What kind of game is the universe playing?"

I look up to see Sam smiling widely, "Well, the universe is clearly setting up opportunities, and you are not grabbing them by the balls. If she bought the trailer and you somehow end up in the same spot meeting multiple times, this is meant to be. So, I'm going to need you to get your feet unstuck from that spot, man the fuck up, go over to the lemonade stand and meet this girl for real and ask her out."

I know he's right. I've had multiple opportunities to connect with this woman, and I keep letting them slip by. But I've been terrified. She's so freaking beautiful and has been so funny and sassy. I'm a little intimidated, and I've never felt this way before. I've always been able to compartmentalize flirting into a sport and leave it at that. But she makes me feel different. I want her. I want to know her, to come close to her and inhale her scent, and ask her how her day was, and have her hold my hand and kiss me softly, asking me what I want for dinner or if I want to take a walk on the beach.

But AGAIN, I don't even know her at all! What are all these things I'm feeling and thinking for a stranger? Trying to ignore the ache in my dick because it's so much more than that, I feel my pulse quicken; it's like an adventure waiting to happen, and I have absolutely no control over it.

I look up from the card and begin to walk again, but I can't see her anymore. In the window of the trailer, two younger servers are busy helping the people waiting in line. Her product is popular, and there is a crowd. But where is she? I looked down for a few seconds; how did she disappear? This place isn't that big. I have to find her. Sam is standing near the trailer holding his arms out straight from his body, indicating, "What the hell, man? You lost her again!"

I look down at the card and take out my cell phone. I type in the number and send a text.

Jake: Well, Ms. Sweet, it appears that the universe wants us to meet again. Where did you go?

Mallory: …

Mallory: …

Mallory: I don't know what is going on. Why are you everywhere I am? Are you stalking me? I'm scared now. You are everywhere.

Jake: Fuck no. I'm not a stalker. We need to meet up and figure this out. Clearly, we are supposed to connect in some way. Can I see you? How did you disappear so fast? Please! Where are you?

Mallory: I don't know about this. I'm not from here. My life is hectic. You're feaking me out right now. And you definitely have interests elsewhere.

Jake: I don't know what you mean. I'm interested in you. What's going on with us? Just meet me to talk. I'm not expecting anything from you (kind of a lie), I want to get to know you. I promise I'm not a stalker. Just let me explain. Did you leave?

Mallory: No, I can't leave. I'm running a business, if you didn't notice.

Jake: Tell me where you are. I need to see you. You couldn't have gone far.

Mallory: This feels dangerous, but I don't see how I can get away. Fine. Come around the back of my trailer.

Jake: Yes! On my way. Don't move!

I head around to the back of the trailer to find her. She's leaning against the side tucked behind a rental freezer, and I can barely see her hair above it, and the toes of her tennis shoes are peeking out. As I come around, I can already smell her lavender scent and the sweetness of

140

her lemonade blend. I cannot shake the want it stirs in me, and I see her turn, looking at me with a shy smile, and she shoves her phone into her back pocket, her back pressed to the trailer. I'm struggling to understand the draw this woman has on me. I come close to her, and I can't resist sweeping a lock of hair from her forehead, out of the way.

Walking close to her, I gently hold her arms, and she looks into my eyes. "Tell me you want to see what this is, and it isn't just me? I can't figure out what keeps drawing us together, but God, I feel like I'm addicted to you, and I don't even know you. I'll step away and leave if you want me to right now. You have to tell me, but I need to taste your lips. Just once. If you'll let me."

She exhales and doesn't break the gaze; she looks confused and intrigued, then nods an almost imperceptible nod.

"Ms. Sweet, I need to hear it. Say it." He growls. "You have to use your words. What do you want to happen right now? If you tell me to, I'll leave now, and it can be like it never happened."

"It's… Mallory, and yes, I want you… this, whatever it is. I want to know what this is about. Yes, please kiss me. Mr. Reyes." She grasps around my neck and pulls me towards her, and that's all I need.

"Jake. It's Jake. And I'm going to kiss you now."

It's all I have thought about regarding this woman, and I crash my lips onto hers. There is nothing gentle or precious about this meeting. We are both hungry animals in need of that first bite after starving for so long. Our mouths are a tangle of lips and teeth and tongues feeding hungrily on the taste of each other. We aren't even a little careful to see if anyone is around, even though we are hiding behind the trailer. Our hands are roaming and grabbing. I push him back, breaking our bond, breathing heavily, holding one hand on his chest and my fingers of my other hand to my lips.

"But what about the woman. From last night? I heard you…" she gasps. He looks confused.

"Uh, Mal…?" A very sweet-looking young server calls tentatively out the door, trying to look anywhere but right at us. She clearly is uncomfortable realizing she just interrupted us.

"Shit. Amelia, sorry! I'll be right there." Mallory answers breathlessly.

"I have to work." She looks at me, confused.

Fuck. FUCK! What am I doing? I'm in public and at a work event. This woman is doing something to me, and I am behaving like a freaking neanderthal. "Yes, of course. I'm sorry."

"No. Don't do that. Don't be sorry because it makes it seem like I attacked you and you didn't want it. Anyway, I've gotta go." She rushes into the trailer.

I'm left standing there, wondering what just happened. And what blonde was she talking about? Bethany? My mind is racing as I try to put all of this together. I can't let this chance slip by. I have no idea what it means, but don't we owe it to ourselves to see?

I text her immediately.

Jake: I need to see you again. Please. To talk.

Mallory: Sir, you can see it's hectic. I leave tomorrow. I don't know if this is a good idea.

Jake: Are you saying it was a bad kiss? You asked me to kiss you. You had to feel that pull together, the heat. You don't want that again?

Mallory: No….yes…I don't know. It was probably the best kiss I've ever had. But let's not ruin it by talking too much, Mr. Reyes.

Jake: Jake. This is not the end. It can't be. I'm not giving up. After all, you did buy my trailer, and according to my friend Sam, we are now forever connected.

18 Mallory

Trying to be professional after having a very steamy make-out session a mere five minutes earlier is something I would not have put on my bingo card for the day, or weekend, or even EVER. Amelia helps me make sure my hair isn't too disheveled and hands me her lip gloss to somewhat cover up my very clearly swollen and deep red lips. Thankfully, I wore my pasties today, or else the crowd would be getting a real up close and personal with my extremely aroused nipples through my tank top.

I step back up to the window as a very sexy and also somewhat disheveled man asks me for a lavender lemonade with Vodka. He smiles, trying to straighten his hair and rumpled shirt front, and fuck if I don't want to throw up my CLOSED sign and take him back out behind the trailer and go right back to where we left off.

"Are you interested…uh…in any information about the business, sir?" I ask him jokingly, slightly out of breath. Jake smiles and rubs his hand across his stubbled jaw, feigning thoughtfulness and piercing me with those gorgeous Superman eyes.

"I am. I'm especially interested in the owner and how she came up with this brilliant business idea. And possibly, if I don't seem too much like a creepy weirdo, she would like to go out with me." He chuckles.

"I'm sorry, Mr.? "I pause, feigning ignorance about who he is.

"Mr. Reyes. Jake Reyes. I'm the person who created this event and…" he looks left and right and leans in to whisper, "just gave you the best kiss of your life. Your words, not mine." He holds out his hand to shake. My eyes go wide, and my cheeks become instantly flushed. He's not wrong, but can he tone it down? I shake his hand lightly, trying not to make too much contact. I cannot handle the electricity I feel in his touch. I smirk and turn to grab his drink. "I'm interested to know what you think about the trailer and my lemonade. Purely professional. Jake."

His eyes get dark when I say his name, and that was not the reaction I was going for. He adjusts his tie, clears his throat, and takes a sip. I'm not trying to flirt with him, but it appears that just the sound of his name on my lips makes him feel things. And I like it. I like seeing him unfold a bit and come a little unglued. I wonder what it would be like if I got on my knees and unzipped his suit pants and sucked him off. What would his eyes look like then? Would he hold my hair and watch or close his eyes and take in the pleasure? Gah! I've never been big on blow jobs, but something about this man was changing my mind.

Snap out of it, Sweet. I try to think of uncomfortable things to get my mind out of his pants and back on actual business—lemon juice in papercuts, flies on rotting meat, moldy raspberries, slimy grocery store sushi. Ok, there. That's better. Focus.

"So, really, what do you think of the trailer? Is it different from what you remember?" I ask.

"This was our family trailer, and I remember what it looked like when you bought it, so yeah, it's very different. You have done a great job. Wow! Coincidentally, I was talking with my mom yesterday about a trip we took in this. But, look what you've done with it! It's just as you described. You really made your dream happen. Congratulations." He offers. Then whispering conspiratorially, "Without the porn." With a sly smile.

I pause, thinking, and then it dawns on me, "Oh my god! That WAS you! I can't believe I said that and that you remembered." I exclaim, "I knew when I heard your voice that first morning at the resort that it sounded familiar. These circumstances are so crazy! This was your family trailer? Did you go camping with your mom and dad? I cannot believe you gave it up for such a steal!"

"Don't remind me." His jaw clenches slightly.

I'm staring at him, trying to imagine him as a scrappy 10-year-old climbing trees, throwing rocks, and roasting marshmallows. My heart beats faster, and I hear a thrum in my ears as I look at the handsome, successful man he has become. I think, if my face were an emoji right now, it would definitely be the heart-eyes one. I have so many fun memories of Jackson and my parents camping when we were kids. My dad was so good at making the campground a party. We never felt like we were roughing it. He always included everyone who would let him. We had contests and games, and played hide-and-seek; anyone who wanted to join was welcome. Those were some of the best times of our young lives. How funny to have met him like this. I wondered if he had similar memories in this trailer.

"Soooo, you guys finally officially met!" Jake's friend walks up and gives him a friendly slap on the back. "It's about fuckin' time! I swear this man cannot stop talking about 'the girl at the massage, the girl at the bar, the girl in the lobby'. And now it's the girl who bought your damn trailer! Can you believe it?"

"We did!" I snap out of my reverie, I smile and look down, doing a terrible job of trying not to give away with the pink of my cheeks and lips what we had been doing only a few minutes earlier.

"Well, that's just great!" he looks back and forth between us with a slightly suspicious glint in his eyes. "You definitely should come hang out with us tonight. Did Jakey tell you my sister is one of the opening acts for Chappell Roan tonight? I can totally get you in."

"Wait, what? That is amazing. Who is your sister?" I ask.

Sam introduced himself earlier when he came to the trailer to get a drink and then hurried off to find Jake, so we didn't really talk much, but now here he was asking me to come hang out with them.

"Ivy Jane!" He does a little dance that I have seen people do on TikTok to one of her songs. I'm laughing, and Jake is just staring at him like he's lost his mind,

"Oh, I have heard her stuff. I love it! How fun! That sounds like so much fun, and congratulations to your sister! Ok, well, I have to see how the rest of the day goes, and I do have to pack up to head back home tomorrow." I say, motioning to my mess in the trailer.

Jake sets his empty container on the ledge and hands me his card. "This was delicious, and I love your stand. I would also love to see you tonight. If you want to, of course. No pressure. Or just come up to my balcony and have a drink. And…"

"Listen to the water?" I chide.

"Yep. That's right. Listen to the water." He laughs, adorably embarrassed.

"I'll text you an update when I'm done here. And thank you for the invite." Looking at both Jake and Sam. "It's great to meet you."

Jake holds out his hand to shake, and when I reach out, the heat when we touch is unmistakable. He holds on just a little longer than necessary, and Sam notices and gives Jake a look. As they turn to walk away, I can see

Sam talking close and quietly to Jake. What are those two up to?

The crowd is dwindling, and I have let one of my servers, Bryce, go home. He has another gig, so he left, and Amelia offered to stay to help me clean up. "You have a hottie waiting for you. Let's get this wrapped up. You can't miss out on that stack of pancakes. He is already all buttered up for you," she waggles her eyebrows.

"Ok, now. Is that what kids are saying these days? I mean, I do like pancakes, but the whole butter thing is a little disturbing. But I could cut into that stack and take a big bite for sure. I guess I already did, and I'm hungry for more, which isn't really like pancakes at all because after pancakes, you are not really hungry for a while," I mumble.

"Girl, you're losing the point here." She stops me. "He's hot and obviously VERY into you. You need to see what that's about. Give him a chance. It seems like you guys have had one too many chance meetings to ignore this. It's time to investigate a little deeper. You deserve to give yourself a chance at happiness, and who cares if it's just one night? But also, what if he's the one?"

"But I heard him with another girl last night. I think he's got a girl at work. Or what if there's more than one? I'm not interested in being one of many sausage links." I cringe as I try to continue the breakfast correlation.

" Ok, ok. No more breakfast comparisons. But let's unpack that. What did you actually hear?" Amelia asks.

I tell her everything from the elevator to the balcony, and what I overheard him saying to her.

"Ok, well, that could mean many things, and from what I saw today, that did not look like a man interested in anyone else. He was all up in your business. Had I not come out to get you, who knows what would have happened?" She side-eyes me with a devilish grin. "Lucky sausage." She walks away laughing.

I laugh. "Ok. You might be right. I'll think about it. Let's get this girl cleaned up."

When we finish cleaning and packing up the trailer, I'm exhausted but so happy. Truly, deeply happy. Days like these confirm in my heart that I've made the right decision to take this leap. A year ago, I was in a very dark place and felt like I might never be happy again. Six months ago, when I lost my job and bought the trailer, it was a defining moment, and to see the light now gives me hope. I thought Adam had broken something in me that might not be fixable.

I haven't felt this content in so long. I know I've made a decision that has genuinely made me look at past events and choices in a new way. A way that makes me start to realize I'm growing. I might not be growing in the ways anyone on the outside would easily notice, but I can feel them in my heart, and that's all I care about. I'm healing. I'm beginning to feel whole again.

I met so many amazing people at the event, who offered loads of good leads on places I can set up my little lemonade stand. This door opening for me is warm and welcoming, and I love it even more because it's all mine. I've created this space for myself to thrive and grow, and I can't wait to see what comes next.

Before I start to drive back to the hotel, I pull out Jake's card and stare at it for at least two minutes. I'm nervous. I begin to shuffle through all the possible 'what if' scenarios, and why would this guy be any different when I look up and see Amelia getting in her car. She catches my eye and pauses. She points at me, knowing exactly what I'm doing, and nods, giving me a thumbs up. I smile sheepishly at her. Damn, I'm easy to read. I shoot her a thumbs-up and type in his number.

Me: Hi, It's Mallory Sweet. I'm just leaving the event space. What time do you think you'll be heading to the concert venue?

Jake: Well, hello, Mallory. I'm so happy to hear from you. We are planning to leave the hotel at 6. Are you in? I would love to have you there. Maybe a cocktail before if you're up for it?

Mallory: Well, Mr. Reyes, that's mighty presumptuous of you. But I suppose I can be ready at 5:30.

Jake: Please call me Jake. Shy face? Really? This from the woman who begged me to kiss her behind a trailer?

Mallory: Okay. I think "begged" is overstating it a bit. You make it sound so dirty and back-alley.

Jake: Haha. Let me have my delusions for a moment longer, please. Not my intention. Don't be embarrassed, please. It was hot, and maybe a little dirty, and back-alley. Which I'm not opposed to. I just wanted to point out that you opened the door, I'm just trying to slide my foot in.

I'm way out of my league here. But I decide to lock in and go for it.

Mallory: I can do a little dirty.

Jake: Oh, my.

Mallory: All right then. I'd love to meet you before. I'll be at the lobby bar at 5:30. What should I wear?

Jake: I'm very much looking forward to it. Wear whatever makes you feel comfortable. I'm sure you can pull off anything.

Mallory: OK! Cow onesie it is! One other question, would it be ok if I invited my friend, Charley? I mean, if it isn't too much trouble. I don't get to see her too often, and she would love this concert.

Jake: I'm sure it's not a problem. I'll text you back if Sam says otherwise. I have no doubt a cow onesie would look amazing on you.

Mallory: You're crazy.

The shower in my room is a welcome solace. The double shower heads pelt me from both sides, and I stand, letting the hot water run over me, melting away the craziness of today. I lather up my hair with the spa shampoo, which takes me back to my random "couples" massage, and I can't help but think about Jake and that hot as fuck kiss we had. I also started thinking about how it probably isn't a good idea to get into someone who lives far from me and clearly has a fan club or "other sausages". But I'm also looking forward to seeing him again and smelling his delicious scent, and I wouldn't mind running my hands through that gorgeous dark hair. I soap up my hands with my body wash, starting with my arms and then running over my breasts. My nipples are hard, I'm not sure if it's from the water or thinking of Jake's tongue against mine, but before I can stop it (not that I want to), my soapy hand has traveled between my legs, and I begin to rub my clit. Thinking of Jake and wishing it were him with his hand, his mouth on my pussy. I lean back onto the wall of the shower and let the feelings and thoughts envelop me. I slide two fingers inside and begin applying pressure to the right spot. I don't worry about the what-ifs or the real-life possibility that I could fall for this guy; I just let my imagination take over. He's there. My hands become his roaming my body, his words envelop me, "Make yourself feel good, Mallory. I want to see you fall apart. Show me how you do it." And within minutes of imagining his lips on mine, calling me by my name in his serious gruff voice, I'm coming. My inner walls are clenching, my upper thighs are tingling, and I'm moaning his name as if I have a right to. As my orgasm subsides, I can't help but smile. I love that I can do that for myself. Don't get me wrong, I want it with another person, preferably a sexy, dark-haired man with strong hands, but it's freaking empowering to know that I can pleasure myself.

I grab my phone from where it's charging on my side table and quickly type out a text to Charley.

Mallory: What are you doing tonight? Last-minute concert with me and my "massage friend" I met at the hotel. I have A LOT to tell you.

Charley: WTF? You have been a busy girl. I can't leave my house until 6. Does that work?

Mallory: Sure, meet us there. I'll send you a pin of the location and let you know when we are on our way. I'll meet you outside with the ticket.

Charley: Oh, how fun! I'm excited to see the concert, but more excited to see your hot man!

Mallory: Um, ok, he's not "my" anything. Weirdo.

Charley: We'll see.

Ugh! I think. What have I gotten myself into for tonight? Well, too late. I'm already heading down to the bar. No turning back now.

19 Jake

Checking my watch for the 50th time, and it's now 5:35. I feel a shift in the room and turn slowly to look at the entrance. Mallory doesn't see me at first, but my god, I see her. She's fucking amazing. She has piled her gorgeous hair in a messy bun with a few pieces escaping and curling around her face. She's wearing an olive-green dress with skinny straps that hits just mid-thigh. Her legs are toned and tanned. I scan all the way down to her sandal-clad feet and see clearly that she likes the sun and is fit as fuck. Her cleavage leaves just enough to the imagination, and hell, if I'm not imagining what her breasts look and feel like in my palms.

My cock is reacting, too. Just a twinge, and I feel the blood flowing straight between my legs. I need to relax and take deep breaths. Let's not scare the girl off before we even get started, buddy. She is scanning the busy bar, and I stand to wave so she can see me. I catch her eyes, and she smiles excitedly, holding her hand in a subtle wave. I let out my breath. I was nervous she would be shy and maybe awkward after our kiss today, but she seems confident and looks good enough to eat. Calm down, Jake. Please get to know her first.

"Well, hello." She pauses, looking me up and down. "Jake, you look very nice tonight." She says softly as she leans in to kiss my cheek. Damn if it isn't sexy the way she says my name like that. I'm happy she finally called me by my first name, although I did get a charge when she called me Mr. Reyes. Is that bossman kink? Something to explore later, maybe. Focus, man. One step at a time.

I'm wearing my black jeans and a dark gray fitted Henley polo. I didn't go overboard on my outfit, but once on a date, the girl told me my ass looked good in these jeans, so I figured, what the hell. Might as well take all the help I can get. I'm not an obsessive gym guy, but I do like to keep in shape and healthy amidst my busy work schedule. I want to think it shows a bit.

"Well, hello. You look good enough to eat." I say, looking her over slowly to gauge her reaction. Her eyes darken and her cheeks flame pink, and I know immediately she hasn't forgotten our kiss, and maybe this means a promise of more kissing. But I'm not going to be presumptuous. I'm going to be a gentleman and get to know her. Yep, exactly that.

She lifts her lashes and looks me in the eyes, "I think we'd better table that discussion for later. Maybe we get to know each other a little first? Slow things down a bit?"

"Of course. You're right. I'm sorry if I made you feel uncomfortable. Would you like a drink?" I ask, pointing to my drink. She looks at my rocks glass and scrunches her nose, "Oh sure, but not that. How about a Rose'?"

Her drink arrives, and we toast and sip, asking the usual questions about where we live and how we ended up here. She tells me about losing her job and seeing the trailer on her drive home.

"I never thought I would actually meet the gruff man on the other end of the phone when I found Amarilla." She explains

"Amarilla?" I ask.

"I named the trailer Amarilla, which is yellow in Spanish because she's such a sunny, sassy yellow girl. Doesn't it fit her perfectly?" She smiles, and it takes everything in me not to reach out and caress her cheek. She's just so lovely and genuine. But I keep my hands to myself, for now. We are slowing it down. A little self-control, Jake, I chastise myself.

I can see how happy this little thing has made her, and it warms me from the inside out. Her genuine joy at having created this space for herself. It reminds me of when I bought my first restaurant and the pride I felt. I knew that I wanted to make something bigger, but that little start was the spark, and I recall the warmth it gave me. Just enough to fuel my fire for my future endeavors. Sometimes I wondered if I had lost that excitement and spark for the company. Had I become jaded and just about filling in my bank account?

I listened to Mallory share how she had lost both her parents and had an excruciating breakup. She wanted to travel but also stay close to home. Her brother and her aunt were essential to her, and she needed to be there for them. This trailer had given her the freedom to move around, see different places, meet new people, and still return to her home base as she desired. I really admired her free spirit, but also her sense of being grounded. Since I didn't have any close family other than Sam, I didn't really know what that felt like. I sometimes felt like an island, and people would stop by, but, by their own choice or perhaps because I pushed them away, would depart. I felt something in the way Mallory talked that I wanted to learn more about her. I wanted to learn her way of living, of being free and yet firmly planted. I hope that she will let me get to know her. I don't have a clue how that would work, but I'm willing to try, for once. But, I think I'm getting ahead of myself.

"Your life now sounds so intriguing," I tell her. "I have lived so long just working for my businesses, I have forgotten what it's like actually to enjoy my work and see the fun in it."

She nods, "Yes, it's so easy to get trapped in the hamster wheel of filling up the bank account and never stopping to look."

I'm confused. "Look? Look at what?"

"Exactly!" She exclaims, "You are so busy you don't even know what to look at. You look at what it is you like about the work. Do you like the food, the locations, your employees, and the customers? Or maybe it's all of it, but you focus on only one of them at a time. Making the food the best it can be, which in turn makes customers happy, which makes employees enjoy what they are doing, and want to do even better. In my case, it's on a much smaller scale, but my goal is to enjoy setting up and seeing the faces of those who stop by to have a drink. They are intrigued by the simplicity of my idea, but also the depth of how it makes them feel. They may remember having a lemonade stand as a kid. They may have a memory of going to a lemonade stand on their roller skates with their dad. Who knows, but those ideas make me want to meet more people and touch more venues. These are the things that fill my heart, and thankfully, it pays the bills, too. Plus, I don't feel like I'm sacrificing time with my family. I can be home when I need to."

"You're brilliant and have a business sense that I couldn't teach. I've seen many people fail in this industry because they don't have that depth of feeling that you just described. I do think it is easy to lose in the busyness and work of it all. I'm glad to hear you seem to have a handle on that now. Hold on to it."

"Thank you. I just knew that if I started this, I would need to be realistic but still have a sense of adventure and imagination."

"Mallory, I can see that you are a truly fascinating person, not just on the outside, because you are fucking gorgeous. I am so glad the universe didn't give up on us getting to have this time together." I hold up my glass. "Cheers to possible chance meetings with new friends."

She holds my gaze for just a few moments too long.

"You think I'm gorgeous?" She blushes.

I move in close. "God, yes. Every time I see you, I have to keep myself from taking you and kissing you again."

And in that moment, I think that she might lean in and close the distance for a kiss, but she holds up her wine glass and toasts, "To friends."

And I feel like someone just popped my favorite balloon. A prick of disappointment deflates my heart. Friends.

Well, at least she's not running and hiding from me this time.

20 Mallory

I've never really shared my feelings and philosophy about working, or why I wanted to start the stand, with anyone. Jackson has heard some of it, but not my true heart, and if he knew that part of it was so I could be around for him, he would probably not be happy. It's not that I think he can't handle life on his own, but I know that if we lost Auntie Mel, he would be lost, too. I can't say precisely why I shared so much, except that he seemed genuinely interested, and the connection of the trailer just made me feel like we needed to have this moment. It felt like a sort of kismet, and I would be denying the obvious fact that something had drawn us together over the last few days, and he deserved an honest explanation of why I needed his trailer and what it meant for my life.

As we finish our drinks, Sam walks in with a huge grin. "Well, lookie here. I'm glad to see you two have finally had a chance to sit and talk."

For some reason, I feel like a teenager who got caught in my room with a boy, and the door was closed. My cheeks flush AGAIN, and he looks between us both. "Did I interrupt something?"

"No, noooo," I say too hurriedly. "We were just sharing business stories."

He doesn't look convinced, but looks at his watch and decides there isn't time to delve into this mystery right now. "Ok, we need to get going. Ivy Jane said we can come by her trailer and say hi if we can get there before 7:30. Let's move!"

I am so excited to meet Ivy Jane and to be here. Who knew a mere week ago that I would have had this fantastic event to boost my little business and make some really cool new friends? I need to remember that—just friends. My heart was telling me a different story, though, as Jake took my hand and led me to the car Sam hired. He opened the door for me, and just before I let my hand go, he placed a gentle kiss on the back of my fingers. I looked at him quizzically. As his eyes met mine, he just shrugged and smiled, "Sometimes friends kiss."

We meet up with Charley at the entrance and head to the trailer. Ivy Jane greets us as though we have known her forever, "Mallory and Charley, right? I'm so glad to meet you!" She is the sweetest girl you could hope to meet. She's two years younger than Sam and looks like a slightly more gorgeous replica of him, but more importantly, she's gracious. She welcomes us with sparkling waters and a snack spread like no other. She laughs, "I always ask for a few snacks, and they go a little overboard. Please help yourselves."

"Thank you so much for letting us come." I gush, "I love your music, and Chappell is just so fun!"

She gives me a big hug and says, "Any friend of Jakey is welcome wherever we are. He's family. So, I guess that means you are, too."

My cheeks heat, I'm slightly stunned and a little uncomfortable. I don't want her to have the wrong idea of Jake and me, and I start to clarify when Jake cuts in.

"Mallory and I actually just met this week at a work event. It's been a crazy set of circumstances. You wouldn't believe everything that happened."

She laughs, "Oh, believe me, Sam has let me in on pretty much everything. And you know how we feel about that? Somewhere, someone wanted you two to meet, and not so that you could have work contacts or go to a concert. There is something to this. Mark my words."

I stuff a cheeseball in my mouth and smile because I have no words. I cannot get involved with this man. And here are his friends already calling me part of the family. I want to run, but I know I can't.

"Where is the restroom, please?" I choke out.

Charley grabs my hand and says, "I know where it is. I stopped on my way in. I'll show you."

As we walk, she stops in front of me, "What is going on, lady? Why are you freaking out?"

"Why am I freaking out? This man is getting inside my head and more importantly, my heart, and I can't do that." I choke out.

"Why can't you? What excuses are you coming up with? Just because you have a drink with someone and go to a concert doesn't mean marriage." She says, looking confused.

"But…we kissed. And it's all I can think about. And he's so sweet and listens to me. We've spent barely any time together, and I want to spend more."

"That is usually how it works, silly. But hold up! You KISSED? When? You didn't tell me this? Tell me everything."

"I saw him at the event, and I panicked because I kept seeing him everywhere, and I thought he was stalking me or something. So, I hid."

"You hid? Like a child? Tell me more." She snorts.

"Listen, this guy had been all up in my business for 3 days, so randomly. I didn't know what was up. It was freaky. But then we texted, and he came to the back of my trailer. I have no idea why it happened. He just held me, and we looked at each other and…"

"Andddd…?" She asks.

"I told him to kiss me." I cringe.

"Oh. My. God. Mallory Lorraine Sweet. You want this man. And you keep fighting it. You asked him to kiss you, and now you're terrified because you liked it and you LIKE HIM!"

"I know! I can't explain what's going on. It's been such a weird connection. We keep literally running into each other and having random meetings. It's as if the universe just won't let up until we make something happen. But I feel like I am out of control. Ever since I bought this trailer, things have gone crazy."

I look at my feet, and she holds the sides of my head, tilting it up, making me look at her. "It's ok if you like him.

It doesn't have to change anything right now. You're not leaving anyone behind or ignoring your responsibilities. Just open yourself up a little. You haven't let yourself really live since Adam, and it's been a year. Perhaps the trailer has magic that snapped you out of your heartbreak and is propelling you forward. Maybe you can have a fun night, and that will be it. It's ok to have a little fun. You deserve to enjoy life, my girl. You know, your business is called 'Squeeze the Day,' and I think it's time you did JUST THAT! Break the seal, my sister! Get some juice out of life."

My eyes well up. "I don't know why breakfast food keeps coming up in reference to this situation, but I'm here for it. You are the best friend. Thank you for being so real. I want to let myself go, but I still feel so let down by 'he who shall not be named' and wonder if it's worth putting my heart out there again. I don't know if I can take another heartbreak, and if I already feel like this about a man I really don't even know, it's sure to feel worse if it ends badly. "

She dabs my eyes with the edge of her sleeve. "No crying. Promise me you will relax and not stress out about this tonight. Just enjoy his company. No one is asking anything else of you. And if he pressures you or hurts you, I'll kick his ass. Now let's go dance our asses off."

We laugh and hug. Heading back to the trailer, I feel better, and I'm going to try. I'm going to live in this moment and enjoy the company of Charley and my new friends. No overthinking. I want to move forward in all areas of my life, but for some reason, this one seems more complicated. I was really hoping my business would become my new first love, but damn if the universe didn't have other ideas.

21 Jake

I've never had a better time at a concert, or at any event that I can think of off the top of my head. Mallory and Charley danced to every song and dragged us guys along. We were Ivy Jane's biggest fans in the front row, and by the time she sang her last song, "Driveway," everyone in our section was on their feet and having the best time. I know Ivy Jane's career is going to skyrocket, and I'm so proud to be able to see it. It doesn't hurt that I get to experience it with a beautiful and fun woman by my side.

I'm trying so hard just to be cool and not stare at her, not touch her every chance I get, but I'm failing. Her smile mesmerizes me, and the pure joy she exudes while she's dancing is contagious. When Ivy Jane sang her ballad "Catch Me If You Can," we swayed to the song. Mallory was standing just a few inches in front of me. I could smell the clean orange scent of her shampoo, and as I watched her move to the beat, I took a chance and came in close behind her, my hands on her hips, pulling her close to me. I leaned in to whisper in her ear, "Is this ok?" She turned, her eyes wide, and smiled, nodding. We moved together to the music, and I felt her melt into me, leaning her head back on my chest. I ran my hands along her sides and wrapped one arm around her, pulling her in even closer. I breathed in her scent and tried to memorize the shape of her body against mine.

I couldn't prepare for what this woman would do to me. I hadn't felt this way in a very long time, maybe not ever, if I'm brutally honest. But I had to tread lightly. She was skittish and committed to the 'just friends' idea. I hope I can change her mind.

I decide to take a chance and lean down to whisper into her ear, "I'm having the best time. You have made this a night to remember. Even if nothing else happens, I wanted you to know that." She laces her fingers in mine and pulls my arms tighter around her. Fuuuck. She's getting harder to resist by the moment.

When the concert ends, we hang out for a while to meet up with Ivy Jane, but she has to get on the road to her bus as they have another concert in Los Angeles in a couple of days. She and the girls exchange phone numbers, and Mallory says she must stop in Ventura on her way up north. I love the way she has just melded into the group of my favorite people.

Sam and Charley seem to have hit it off, talking about everything from their love of old movies and TV shows to places they haven't traveled yet but want to.

"Who's up for a nightcap?" Sam asks as we head to the car, and Charley raises her hand, "Absolutely, me please! We need to toast to a fucking fantastic night. Thank you so much for making it possible for me to come with you. I have listened to your sister, but seeing her live was next level. I'm sure she's gonna be a very busy girl in no time." Sam high-fives her and says, "Lady, you're one of us now. No going back." Charley whoops, and they walk off hand in hand, laughing.

I look at Mallory, incredulous. "What is going on there?" She shakes her head, "I have no clue, but it seems our besties have just become besties. It's good. Charley has had a rough patch recently. She needed a night to let loose." We chuckle.

"Do you want to go get a drink? No pressure. I know it's been a long day for you," he says.

"You putting me to bed, dad?" she chides, knocking into me with her shoulder.

I smirk, my eyes going dark, and my voice husky, "First of all, if I were putting you to bed, you wouldn't have to ask, you would know. And do not call me 'dad'. It sounds creepy."

She softly pokes me in the side, joking, "Oh no, daddy is getting frustrated. How about Mr. Reyes?"

I grab her hand and turn her towards me, pulling her against my body, growling, "Oh god. That's worse! I am

NOT your daddy. If you want me to put you to bed, I will, and if you need it, there might be spanking involved."

Even in the dark, I can see her look is heated, and her breath hitches. She places a hand on my chest and slowly drags it down towards the waistband of my jeans, then slides it around to my butt, pulling me to her and whispers closely in my ear, "Are you threatening me with a good time? Because I think I might like that. Please. Put me to bed. Can I call you Mr. Reyes?"

This woman has a hold on me. I press myself against her and lean down so my lips brush her ear, "As you wish."

Sam and Charley are in the car, giggling together. "Come on, you two! The night isn't getting any younger."

I lean into the car and tell them to go on ahead, and that Mallory is tired and we're going back to the hotel. They both roar with laughter and shout "Get a roooom!" I can hear them both chime in, "I knew it!" And I'm sure my face is red.

I shut the door and turn to Mallory, who holds up her phone and has already ordered a car that's 4 minutes away.

As they drive away, she shivers, "I'm sorry. Are you cold?" I ask. She snuggles up close to me, and I wrap my arms around her. "A little," she says, and tilts her face up to kiss me on my neck. I look down, questioning. I'm still not totally sure where this is going. I mean, I know she asked me to put her to bed, but does she mean like tuck her in and say goodnight? Like literally? I'm so out of practice of reading signals; maybe she wasn't being seductive. Because what I really want is to strip that dress off and worship that glorious body of hers. I have been thinking about it for 3 days nonstop, and fuck, it's going to be a sad night if I have to leave her without even a taste.

She smiles mischievously, "Sometimes friends kiss." I laugh and hold her tight.

"You are truly something, Ms. Sweet."

"You're not so bad yourself, Mr. Reyes." She whispers.

Aaaand, I'm getting hard. Damn, this girl pushes all my buttons.

22 Mallory

He winds his hand into mine, interlocking our fingers as we drive. His fingers on his other hand brush along my thigh at the hem of my skirt. God, I love his hands. They are strong and move with confidence, but still soft and gentle. The gentle skim across my leg only makes me want them all over my body. The electricity between us is palpable, and my skin prickles under his touch. I wonder if the driver can sense it, because I'm convinced it has replaced all the air in the car, and I can barely breathe. My heart is surely beating a million beats per minute, and if he looked, I swear he'd be able to see it. I'm trying not to look, but it looks like the zipper area of his jeans is pretty tight. Did I do that? I really hope so. Knowing that a mere touch can cause his body to respond that way makes me feel confident and assertive. He exhales and adjusts his position in his seat, and now I'm sure he feels it, too. Is it possible that after just a couple of days of knowing someone, I could feel a connection this strong? I'm seriously losing control, and I'm not even that scared. But I have to know something first, so I dive in.

"Jake, can I ask you something?" I lean on his shoulder.

He breathes out and seems to be preparing for a deep, introspective question.

"Sure. I'm ready."

I laugh, "Oh, you are? You think you are ready for this question?"

He looks nervous. "Well, now I don't know. You're scaring me."

So, I take a deep breath and out with it. "Are you sleeping with or in a relationship with that blonde that works with you?"

His eyes go wide, and he looks at me quizzically. "Why would you think that?"

"Well, why wouldn't I? She's hot and gorgeous. You are hot and gorgeous. It would make sense. Aaaand I may have overheard you and her on your balcony the night I saw you in the elevator, and you invited me to your room. It sounded like you already had plans in your room with her. I don't want to become part of some triangle. I already ended up in one of those unwillingly, and it's not really my thing." I explain.

"You lost me at you think I'm hot and gorgeous. Please repeat everything you said after that." He smiles a broad, cheeky smile.

Now I'm getting worried. Why isn't he just refuting it if nothing is going on? What's the delay in explanation? Am I making something out of nothing? If so, he should say so.

"Why are you deflecting? This situation feels icky. If something is going on with you two, it's fine. We're not that invested here. I just met you, and no hard feelings, but

I just can't get involved with that. I need to know. I've been down this road before. I'm not going to be the second choice to anyone ever again. Are you just trying to fuck me and add me to a list? I'm not about that life, if that's the case." I blurt.

He leans his head back on the headrest and laughs so loudly. "Ohhhh, now who's the creeper?"

It pisses me off. "Why are you laughing? It's not funny?"

He holds my hand tighter and places his other hand on my cheek, turning me to face him.

I keep my eyes downward, having a hard time looking at him.

"Whoa. Mallory, look at me. I'm sorry. I was laughing because this could not be further from the truth." He says, caressing my cheek with his thumb, "I am not in a relationship with, nor am I fucking my PA. I will tell you whatever you want to know. I'm not hiding anything. Her name is Bethany. I won't lie: she's been crushing on me, but I have told her it's not going anywhere. She understands this. Unfortunately, you overheard her latest attempt to get me to get together with her on the balcony. I said no and escorted her to her room. I went back to my room, and we have NEVER slept together or had any romantic physical contact. And to your other question, I don't have a list. I haven't even been on a date in over a year. My work life tends to take precedence over dating. I'm not about that life either. You are the first woman to catch my eye in so long. You are captivating, and I want to spend more time with you. That's all. I think the universe wants it, too. Don't you? Think about the last few days. We end up at the same resort, then in a weird couple's massage scenario, and the business event, MY event, where you show up in a trailer you bought from ME. And who are we to deny it what it wants? And if you let me kiss these gorgeous lips again, that's entirely enough. Ok?"

I exhale with relief. That's all I needed. His soft and honest explanation is enough to give me butterflies. He's not wrong; it does seem wild that all of these things could just be a coincidence. My resolve is waning because his tender touch on my cheek and sweet words have made my nipples hard and my panties wet. I want this. Whatever it is.

"Ok," I say, I look up, realizing we are at the hotel, and the driver is tapping his steering wheel and peering at us in the rearview mirror, waiting for us to get out. We laugh nervously.

"Oh god! Sorry!" I say to the driver, and we hurriedly slide out.

Jake places his hand on the small of my back and leads me to the elevator.

As soon as the door closes, I can't stop myself. I turn to him and, standing on my tiptoes, go up for a kiss. He reaches under my dress and cups my butt cheeks with those gorgeous hands, lifting me off the ground. My god, the muscles are not just for show. I wrap my legs around him and run my fingers into the strands of hair at his neck, pulling him closer, deepening our kiss. Our lips crash, and our tongues are eagerly tasting and feeling. I grind my center on his cock that is definitely creating a sizeable bulge in his jeans. We don't have long, it's only on the 3rd floor, and just as we hear the ding, we pull apart, and he lowers me gently, as we try to regulate our breathing. Thankfully, no one is waiting to enter at this hour. I straighten my dress, and we walk out as if we aren't slightly disheveled and flushed.

As the door to his room closes, he immediately turns me and presses me against the door, holding my hands above my head. "Are you ready for me to put you to bed, Mallory?" He says in a low voice into my hair. His breath is warm, and his words sink into my soul, and I understand his meaning. My nipples are tight, and the ache between my legs begins to creep up into my lower back. His free hand is under my dress, rubbing a slow circle on my ass. I feel an urgency to make him do more.

"What happens if I sass you?" I squeak out.

"Try it." He baits me.

I'm not sure what will come from this. I don't usually play like this, but he's got me so turned on I can't help myself. I've never been in the situation before. Everything feels so raw and exposed. His scent, the feel of his hands, the pronounced bulge pressing into my low back, and the promise of seeing the rest of him are intoxicating, and I want more. I need all of it. Come what may. I haven't felt this way in a very long time.

"You can't tell me what to do, Mr. Reyes." I taunt, fluttering my eyelashes and then staring directly into his eyes like a petulant child, and just to top it off, bite my lip and press my hips back into his cock.

His chuckle is deep, sexy, and just slightly menacing. "You asked for it, Ms. Sweet." He runs his hand up and down my side, brushing the edge of my breast and allowing one finger to brush lightly over my nipple, making my breath hitch. He slides it down slowly and then makes a couple more soft circles with his palm on my ass and gives it a solid smack. Not too hard but just enough to make a sound and send electricity straight to my pussy. I cry out, "Oh fuck, Jake. Yes. You're making me so wet."

"Oh my god, Mallory." He breathes, reaching down between my legs. "Fuuuck, you are soaked. So hot. You are so damn sexy. You are ready for me, and I love it."

I have no idea who this person is right now. I am in another realm of chasing pleasure, and this man has awakened something in me that I never knew existed. It feels like an awakening to the desires I have tamped down and not allowed myself to realize. The pain of my last relationship has made me so afraid and cautious; I haven't allowed myself to feel anything. But fuck, I'm feeling EVERYTHING right now. My body is on alert and desperate for this man.

"So much." I pant, "I need more. Please, I want you so badly." And I press my backside into his hard cock again.

I feel him kneel behind me, running his hands down my thighs, and he lifts my skirt. His hands rub my ass again, and then he slowly pulls my panties down, kissing each ass cheek gently.

"You didn't say anything about my panties. Do you like them?" I whisper, and he pauses and chuckles.

He stops and slowly slides them back up. "My apologies. Did you wear these for me, Mallory? Were you hoping I would end up here?"

They are a sheer black fabric with embroidered green vines all over the front.

"I...I wasn't sure. But yes, I hoped." I respond, suddenly feeling timid.

His voice comes out gruff. "Come on, don't get shy on me now. Be a good girl, Mallory. It makes me crazy hearing you call my name." He runs his palm to my belly and runs it down, feeling the dampness between my legs. "Damn, I want this wet pussy immediately. I need to know what you taste like. I need these panties gone. May I?" He asks while softly running his nose up and down my slit.

"Fuck Jake, you don't have to ask anymore. I consent. To all of it. Please. I need your tongue." I moan.

"God, you look so hot. You dress up around your waist, and that gorgeous ass is waiting for my mouth. Please tell me again what you want. I want to hear you say it." I tease.

"Oh my god. I need your tongue in my pussy and on my clit. Please, put your beautiful mouth on my pussy and make me come on your tongue!" I plead.

I don't know who I have become in these last moments, but I like her. I like the way this man has begun to release me from my self-imposed prison of denial. I have denied myself what I want and need for long enough. I'm ready to break free, and Jake is making that possible.

He stays behind me, leaning me over while his talented tongue licks from back to front in slow, languid strokes, flattening his tongue, making the most glorious sounds. With my ass arched back towards him, he spreads me open and alternates licking and sucking on my clit, bringing the bundle of nerves to life. My legs begin to quiver, and I feel the beginning of my climax quickly start to grow low in my belly and between my legs. He pauses to kiss gently along the outside of my pussy. "Are you ok?" He asks quietly. "I'm so okay, but I'm not sure how long I can stand here. You are making me weak. My legs are like jelly." I confess, breathing heavily.

"Well, now, I don't want to stop, but I can't have you uncomfortable when I make you come." He wipes his hand across his mouth, smiling devilishly as he turns me around and kisses me, allowing me to taste myself, making my arousal skyrocket. He lets my skirt drop and then unzips the back. I let the straps fall off my shoulders, and the dress falls to the ground. I feel a little awkward having no bra on, but I am wearing little nipple cover circles. He laughs, "I wondered why I never could see those amazing nipples poking out tonight." I peel them off, and he takes a sharp inhale.

"My god, Mallory, I can't believe I'm so lucky. You are fucking gorgeous." I'm not good at taking compliments and deflecting.

"Take your shirt off, please," I ask. He obliges without question, grabbing the back of his neck and pulling it off in one motion, and who knew shirt removal could be so hot. I bite my bottom lip, looking at his glorious form. His body is beautiful. He's fit and tan and has a little trail of hair running down into his jeans that is beckoning me to find out what's under there. I run my hand down his chest, feeling very empowered, and he feels like fire and ice all at the same time. The mere touch of him is lighting me up, and his darkened gaze makes me shiver.

He firmly takes my wrist, stopping me. "Now, let's not get distracted. I was in the middle of a delicious meal, and you interrupted me." He scoops me up and carries me to the bed. "On your hands and knees, Mallory." He directs. I crawl onto the bed, facing the headboard, and glance back at him. He's looking at me as though he cannot decide exactly what he wants to do with me.

He runs his hand down my side. "God, what a beautiful sight. You're perfect. I cannot wait to have that pussy from behind. Not yet, though." He slides in under me on his back, placing his hand on my hips, pulling me into him. "Now, please sit on my face so I can continue eating that glorious pussy." He commands.

And I'm coming undone. This man and his beautiful, dirty mouth have taken hold of me, and all I can do is whimper, writhe, and moan. He licks and sucks and slides a finger up and inside, applying pressure in just the right spot, and I swear I see heaven when I feel my orgasm begin to build. "Oh god, right there. Please, more!" I beg. He releases pressure and slows the motion, and the loss is almost too much to bear, and I cry out, "No! Why?"

"Not yet, baby. Let it build. I promise it will be worth it. There is so much more for you." He assures.

In a soothing voice, he whispers, "Do you want more?" I can barely comprehend language at this moment, but I think I say something like "all of it".

He chuckles, "Greedy girl, I see," and slowly adds another finger, increasing pressure inside and flattening his tongue, adding more pressure on my clit, and within what feels like seconds or hours, I have no perception of time or reality, I'm gone. My release is coming upon me in waves of pleasure from deep in my belly down my legs, and I'm holding the headboard for dear life.

I cannot contain my words, "Jake! Fuck yes! Oh God, Jake! So fucking good!" I call him. It lasts what feels like forever, and he is unrelenting, holding me in place on his mouth until he squeezes every drop out of me. I collapse and begin to slide down to kiss him. His lips are slick with the evidence of my orgasm, and it's so hot. He did that for me. I've never felt anything so deeply and completely encompassing. He has ruined me.

"What sorcery was that? You have a magic mouth." I say breathlessly.

He chuckles, vibrating my head on his chest, and it's such a lovely, deep sound that makes my heart swell. Oh fuck. I like this man. "I'm glad you feel that way. Because I'm very much looking forward to doing it again, soon," he says.

In this moment of vulnerability, I slide my hand to his waistband and begin fumbling with his jeans. After I struggle for a minute, he helps me by unbuttoning and unzipping them and lowering them enough that I can slide them off the rest of the way. I look up at him, and his eyes are dark, and his pupils dilated. I would ask him if it's ok, but I can see that it is more than ok.

I run my hand over the bulge in his boxer briefs, not pulling them off yet. His breath is a hiss, and he props his head up to see me. I look at him again and squeeze his length through the briefs, and he widens his legs just a bit. I take this as a request to do more. I gently run my fingers under the waistband and start to slide them down, allowing his cock to be released. And oh, my, is it a lovely sight to see. It is hard and heavy, jutting towards his stomach and ready for me to enjoy. He lifts slightly so I can take his underwear off completely, and as I do, I marvel at this beautiful man. I slowly run my hands up his legs and over his thighs, pausing at the apex. I slide one hand under to cup his balls, and he jumps slightly with a soft "uff" and then relaxes into my touch.

Now, if I'm being honest, I'm not a worshipper of the penis. I appreciate it for its use in creating magic in the bedroom, and I appreciate my own ability to mesmerize a man with my mouth on it. But the actual look and feel have never held my admiration until today. This man has a beautiful cock. It's just so proportionately long and big. It doesn't scare me, but it seems just right. Am I the Goldilocks of dicks? No. I haven't had THAT many to compare, but this is a freaking nice one. And I have to tell him.

"Your dick is gorgeous." I declare, feeling emboldened by the serotonin running through my veins.

He laughs until tears fill his eyes and says, "Well, I love that you think so. I don't think anyone has ever complimented me quite that way before. I know who to call if I need a hype person."

"No, really. I mean, I'm not trying to get sidetracked here, but I've really never seen one that I think is so nice, and maybe it's because I'm going to get to put it in me soon, but geez, you've got the goods, my friend." I continue.

He smiles, pulls me to him, and kisses me deeply and tenderly, taking his time. "While I love the praise, I think we might be losing the moment."

"Oh, sorry," I say sheepishly. "I just felt you should know, but yes, let's get back to that. I'm really excited to put my mouth on your cock right now. Excuse me." I slide back down, smiling up at him, wrapping my hand around him, and reveling in the fact that he's still very hard, and his breath quickens. I slide and twist my hand gently and then lower my mouth a little at a time, keeping my eyes on his. I use the moisture from my mouth to continue sliding my hand and twisting around it gently. His mouth opens slightly, and I hear a low guttural grunt. Yes, I'm going to enjoy making this man come.

"Damn. If someone had told me this morning this would be how my evening ended, I would have called them crazy." He breathes.

"Are you disappointed?" I take him all the way out of my mouth to chide him.

"Oh god no. Please. don't let me distract you." He begs

I return him to my mouth, licking circles over the head, and then continue to suck and twist my hand up and around. I draw him in again all the way to the back of my throat, keeping an eye on his reaction. He wraps a hand in my hair and starts to move my head up and down gently, and I let him. I then move between his legs and set to work listening to his moans and feeling my own wetness and arousal between my legs.

I pause, sliding his cock from my mouth with a pop, surprising me and making me laugh shyly, then ask him, "Do you want to come in my mouth?"

He responds by pulling me up to him, kissing me deeply, "My god, woman. What a question. I'd love nothing more, but I really want to fuck you. If that's ok?"

I'm surprised by him kissing me after having him in my mouth. I'd always thought men hated that. It makes me want him even more.

I swear, I'm going to come just by his words. I nod, and he flips me over to my back. Straddling me, he cups my breasts, massaging them. "Now, if we want to talk masterpieces…your breasts are fantastic and stellar." He lowers his mouth to take my nipple in licking and sucking gently, then switches to the other one. He licks and sucks back and forth, stopping for a moment to pinch them. My eyes close and my back arches, urging him on, and I'm on the verge of another orgasm. "You're going to make me come, just with that," I say. He smiles and keeps going. He leans in to kiss me, "Hold that thought." He quickly moves off of me and into the bathroom.

I hear him rifling through his bag, and when he returns, condom in hand, I spread my knees and lick my fingers and then put my hand between my legs, rubbing my clit, showing him how ready I am. He doesn't take his eyes off me as he rolls on the condom.

"My god, Mallory, you are so hot. How did I get so lucky to find you? Please keep doing that, baby." He says as he climbs back on the bed.

"Mr. Reyes. Please put that art piece of a cock inside me now." I order.

He laughs. "Of course, Ms. Sweet. Since you asked so politely."

He drags his length across my wet pussy, and I moan. "You're so wet." He groans.

"That's what that gorgeous cock does to me. I'm so ready." I respond.

He begins to enter me slowly, inch by inch, and I arch up, lifting my hips and wrapping my legs around him, trying to take him in. "Take it slow, baby. I want to feel every bit of you." And he begins to thrust, slowly at first.

"So. Freaking. Good. Jake." I say haltingly between each delicious thrust. He begins to quicken his pace. He pulls one of my legs up over his shoulder, creating space to go deeper, and my god, it's perfect. He is completely seated inside me, and I have never felt so perfectly full. We are two pieces of a machine moving in unison, creating heat with the friction of our bodies. The rhythm is a song that we are singing together, and we are in perfect harmony. I cannot ever remember a sexual experience that has felt so good both mentally and physically. I really wasn't expecting another orgasm; it's not something that usually happens for me during sex, but I feel it building. "I'm going to come again already," I tell him, slowing him and looking into his eyes. "You feel so amazing. I don't want to come yet, but you feel so fucking good, I don't know how long I can hold on," he breathes. He pulls himself almost all the way out, pausing, and I pout, "Aww, where did you go?" As he slowly lowers himself and slides his cock back in, he groans, and after what might have been minutes or hours, we are coming, his pleasure playing out across his face. And his voice rasps out a quiet curse of pleasure. "Fuck, Mallory. You feel so good." He's kissing me, and all at once, we are in a satiated pile and holding each other, panting and slick with sweat. And I am mesmerized.

I try my best not to slip from this place of ecstasy and enjoy the pure peace of the calm after the terrific storm. I have to breathe deeply and focus myself on the moment. My brain desperately wants to slip into overthinking mode.

He rolls to the side to look at me, and our eyes lock, and because I just can't shut the fuck up and enjoy the moment, I say, "That dick deserves a Nobel Peace Prize."

He laughs, shaking his head, and places a kiss on each of my breasts and a light smack to my ass, before heading to the bathroom to discard the condom. As I watch him walk away, I can't help but smile and curl into myself in total satisfaction. He returns with a wet, warm washcloth for me, and just that simple little gesture has me lit up inside. I've confirmed, I'm too easy.

23 JAKE

On my way back from the bathroom, I take a detour by the fridge and grab two glasses and a bottle of champagne. As I return, I see Mallory is wearing one of my t-shirts and is standing at the open patio door. And fuck if she doesn't look delectable. Her ass cheeks are peeking out from the bottom, and she's piled her hair up in a messy bun. I step in behind her, wrapping my arms around her. "I know we need to get some sleep, but I wanted to look at the water. Since that's what you actually invited me for." She says with that signature smart-aleck tone.

"You know what, sassy?" He says, giving me another light smack on the ass, "I didn't hear any complaints a few minutes ago. Actually, I heard a LOT of compliments about my grade A cock."

"True, true. But I do love the water. I should probably go soon, though," she says and slips away to start gathering her clothes.

I grab her gently by the arm. "What are you doing? Where's the fire? Let's sit out here and have a glass of champagne. And, you don't have to leave. Stay with me tonight. Please?"

She looks up at me, "I don't know…" the uncertainty of the moment on her face. I can tell she's ready to bolt, and I want to do anything to make it stop. Whatever her fears are, they are starting to seep out again.

"Listen, Mallory," I say, gently taking her dress and shoes from her and setting them on the chair. "I know we don't know each other well, but this has been one of the most amazing nights I've ever had with anyone. I'd really like to spend a little more time with you. I'm not asking for anything else. Just an hour? Can we do an hour, and then if you are ready to go back to your room, we will say our goodbyes and call it a night? What do you say?"

She looks uncertain. "Just one hour?" she questions nervously.

"Yes," I say, and then gather her in my arms. "Besides, you look really sexy in my t-shirt, so I'm going to need to look at you wearing it for just a little longer."

We head out to the balcony, and before she can sit on the other chair, I pull her onto my lap. She seems stiff at first, but I put a finger to her chin and draw her close for a chaste kiss. "I think this is where you belong." And I think I mean my lap, but it feels like there is so much more that I'm not saying, and at this point, neither one of us is brave enough to acknowledge. She sighs and sinks into me, and we look out at the darkness toward the ocean, and it feels like the crashing waves are speaking volumes, engraving this moment on our hearts. No matter what happens next, we have changed each other these last few days.

"Soooo, maybe we get to know something about each other in this hour? Nothing deep, just conversation. What do you think?" she asks shyly.

"I can do that. Anything off limits?" I say softly and squeeze her close. The need to touch this woman as much as possible before she leaves is closing in around me. I hope she doesn't feel my desperation.

"No questions about exes." She taps her chin. "And, no trauma bonding."

"Ok. Let's get started. But first, a toast." I open the champagne and pour, handing her a glass.

"Cheers to an amazing time with an amazing person." I lift my glass.

She lifts hers, and we clink. "AND amazing orgasms!" She adds laughing,

"Ok. You'd think I was prepared by asking for this, but I'm not. Let's see, how about this: if you have to drive somewhere and you can take the freeway or backstreets, which do you choose?" Mallory says.

"Really? That's the burning question you have?" I chuckle.

"I didn't say it was 'burning' questions. I just said getting to know each other." She smacks my chest. "This is good information. It tells me a lot about how you choose to live life. Now - answer."

"Ok. Fine. There are things that affect this answer, though. But if I think of just jumping in the car and going to my favorite beach spot, I'll take the back roads. The views on the way are fantastic. Which, I guess, leads me to: most often, if I can take a scenic route, I will. Unless I'm in a hurry or racing Sam or my dad to get somewhere because they always think they know the fastest way to get everywhere." I finish.

"Wow. Mr. Reyes. That was a very in-depth answer to a simple question." She chides.

"Well, there are different places that require a different frame of mind. You wanted to get to know me, right? It's not like you asked my middle name. Now that would be straightforward." I respond.

"Ooohhh," she says excitedly, clapping her hands, "What IS your middle name?"

"No way, lady," I scoff. "That's two questions. It's my turn."

"Ugh. Ok fine. Shoot." She concedes.

"If you could have a superpower, what would it be?" I ask with a wiggle of my brows.

"Aha. Quintessential 'getting to know you' question. I like it. So, you would think something like invisibility, or flight, but you would be wrong." Setting her glass down, she begins rubbing her hands together.

"What? Everyone wants to be invisible! What could be better? To go wherever you want and no one would know?" I argue.

"Hear me out. Shape shifting!" She says confidently, pressing a hand to my chest

I bark out a laugh. "Ok. This should be interesting. Please elaborate."

She stands up to face me, "Ok, get ready to have your mind blown, because I've really thought about this. Here goes. What people forget is that all of those superpowers, not including teleportation or telekinesis, can all be solved by shapeshifting. People usually think it limits them to animals, but it really doesn't. You can shape-shift into anything you want to. Invisibility? Chameleon or octopus. Strength? Bears, lions, gorillas, and more. Speed? Cheetahs, gazelles, or even a rabbit! Some lesser-wanted powers can also fall under shapeshifting, like elasticity, agility, elemental control, or at least redirecting. Vampirism, size manipulation, and loads more can be done with shapeshifting alone. Shapeshifting doesn't limit you to what currently exists, but limits you to pretty much anything, real or fake, past, present, or future. Nobody ever specified the limits of that ability; for example, nobody said you couldn't shapeshift into something with pyrokinesis, teleportation, or necromancy. So, my conclusion is that shapeshifting ability is pretty much limitless, and the shapes one could take are infinite." She folds her arms in front of her and looks at me with a smug smile.

I am stunned and impressed all at once. I reach up gently from my seated position to unfold her arms and pull her back down to me. As she is settling back on my lap, I take her chin and turn it towards me, kissing her gently. I can't quite place the look in her eyes when she looks at me after the kiss. It feels heavy and almost too vulnerable for how long we've known each other. "You know, I'm not sure if I'm turned on or scared. I think that might be slightly unhinged, but it actually makes sense to me. I love that you have thought this through so in depth. It's very impressive in a very nerdy way. How did you come up with that?"

I hold his gaze, and even in this silly conversation, it feels like we've landed in a very intimate space. "My brother and I are very close in age, and he was so into superheroes and comics. I learned a lot, and we had many conversations about this. He's critical to me, and I guess this stuff makes me feel closer to him. Because our parents were older, we had to find ways to entertain ourselves. And now that they are both gone, even though we still have our aunt, we are all each other has and these memories. I know it seems silly, but we have fun. Tell me you wouldn't want to be a cheetah at some point, or maybe your boss's desk so you can hear all the shit he's talking about you." She says.

"Well," I chuckle, "First, I don't think it's silly at all. I love that you have that with your brother. Second, I am the boss, so maybe I would want to be a piece of equipment in one of my restaurants to hear all the scuttlebutt amongst my employees."

"Scuttlebutt?" she snorts, covering her mouth. "What are you, 80? No one says scuttlebutt, Jake. My advice, don't ever say that word in front of your employees or you definitely WILL be the talk of the breakroom."

"I'm 32, Miss Sweet. What should I say -'tea'? How old are you?" I scoff.

"No, please don't say tea. That's not a good look for you either. Maybe stick with 'gossip'. Universal word and ageless. And, I'm 30." She responds like a child, so proud to have her birthday. "Anyway, I feel like we got derailed here. You know way too much about me, now. Tell me about your business. How did it start?"

I hesitate, "You really want to know that? It might be boring to you. You sure?" He asks.

I nod, "I'm a budding businesswoman. I need to glean all I can from the venerable restaurant king. Plus, I don't think you could be boring if you tried. Remember, prize-winning dick?" She bites her lower lip, looking at me with wide eyes.

"Ok, let's not get crazy with the 'venerable' stuff. And be careful, Ms. Sweet. Keep talking about my prized dick and biting that damn lip, and we'll end up doing way less talking and back to fucking. Especially since you are sitting here in just a t-shirt. I'm barely holding on, knowing your beautiful bare ass is right there with nothing covering it."

She laughs and clears her throat, folding her hands in her lap. "Ok, sorry. I'll behave. Go ahead."

I continue. "I have had some success. And I will tell you why in a minute. So, I started with a small bar that I built and grew into my first restaurant. I never really had the vision or dream to have multiples, but people reached out to me because they liked what I had created and wanted me to help them create a similar vibe. The original bar is now the restaurant in Laguna. I bought the bar when I graduated from college. I had bartended there and saved every penny to do it. The owners were a lovely older couple, and we became close when I worked there. They knew I needed a safe space and that my parents were not close by, nor did they have the money to help. So, when I graduated, they had decided they wanted to retire and sell it to me. They had one condition. I had to maintain the vibe of the bar, even though they knew I wanted to make it a beachside restaurant; they didn't want me to lose the casual everyman vibe. So much of the area has turned bougie, and we really wanted to make sure everyone felt welcome there. A cozy beach vibe that's not just for people with a big bank account. And that's my secret. Keeping things real. Jobs for locals and an atmosphere that fits everyone. If you want to dress up and have a fancy night or roll in casual and sandy for an after-beach bite, this is the place."

She sighs, "I love that so much. I feel like so much of what I'm doing has that same goal behind it. I'm worried, though, that I'm going to end up at bougie birthday parties and not hanging out with fun people who really want to support my business."

"I hear you," he says, "but the key is that you will have some of that, and to leave room for it because they will get your name out there, but that will allow you to do more of the kinds of things you actually want to. Does that make sense? You don't have to write off one to have the other. Let it fuel your real desires and goals. Just make sure you don't lose that along the way. That's the hard part. Staying grounded. But I think you have good friends who will help you keep your eyes on what you really want. And…" He starts to say something else, but stops short. "Well, anyway, that's it. Just stay true to yourself."

"What were you going to say?" She asks.

"I don't want to say too much. I might freak you out." He responds.

"Well, now you are for sure." Her eyes squint slightly, and she's got a questioning look on her face.

"Ok," He says, "I just wanted to say, and now you've got me as a resource. I want you to feel like you can use me and ask me anything about the business. I would be honored to help you be successful in any way I can. No pressure."

Her eyes go wide, "Wow. That's very generous of you. But, don't you charge like $200 an hour for consultation? Also, with offers like that, how do you stay grounded and not lose what you wanted in the beginning?"

I take a more serious tone. "Honestly, that's a tough question to answer right now. I have been doing a shit job of it. With five locations to juggle as well as trying to do marketing events like this, I'm running myself to the edge, and it's going to blow up in my face soon if I don't get control. I love what I do, and when I see an opportunity to grow and expand, I can't resist. I forget that I need to delegate more and trust those I've hired to do their jobs well. I've built a great team with superior systems in place, but I get nervous."

"Nervous? You always seem so confident and sure of yourself," she questions.

"I don't want to let anyone down. I've got so many people depending on this business to feed their families. I get freaked out thinking about anything going wrong, and I'm constantly trying to think one step ahead. The restaurant business can be unstable. One minute you have the hottest spot in town and the next you're shuttering the windows. This is why I try to keep the properties timeless. Right now, it's working, but I'm always living in the what-if. I know it's not healthy. I've just accepted it as my normal now." I confess

I sit silent for a beat and then breathe out a laugh, trying to lighten the mood, "Whoa. That got heavy. Anyway, the offer was a friends-and-family-only discount. Or you can just keep complimenting my enormous cock."

"Um, I don't think I used the word 'enormous'. Let's not put words in my mouth." She laughs.

"Ok, ok, sorry, I believe you said 'work of art'." I pull her in close, whispering in her ear. "And if we keep talking about it, it's going to be hard again, and I'm going to want to put more than words in your mouth, and consequently, we might go over your hour. But seriously, I do have one more question. If that's ok?"

"Shoot." She says, looking at me, her face so open and honest. It's almost disarming.

I pause, taking her in and trying to figure out how to get her to stay without scaring her, then go ahead with my question. "What does the tattoo on your neck mean? Who is Dianne?"

She smiles. "You noticed that??"

He smirks, "I was pretty up close and personal with you just a bit ago, in case you forgot."

"Oh no, I did NOT forget. It's just small, so a lot of people don't notice it." She says, smiling, rubbing my chest.

She leans against my chest and begins. "Ok. It's simple but full of meaning. Dianne is my mom's name. Or was. I'm never sure how to say that. Anyway, she was my best friend, besides Jackson. We could laugh about anything, and my dad would pretend to get irritated with us because we would fall into a giggle fit and couldn't stop.

If we let it go too far, anything would make us laugh. We took a road trip once to meet up with an old friend of hers from high school. We drove, or I should say I drove, all the way to Austin, Tx. We had the best time. We decided before we went that we would stop at any roadside attraction we wanted and eat all the crap snacks our hearts desired. She didn't want to drive because the freeway made her nervous, so I took the road.

She had started to lose her hearing in her left ear, so every time I would say something, she wouldn't hear me. It was frustrating, but it became funny. I would try to have a conversation, and she would look at me with a cringey smile, feeling bad because she didn't hear me. I couldn't be mad at her because she hated getting older and having her body fail her. We decided to pull off and go to Tombstone, AZ, otherwise known as the "Town too Tough to Die", the home of the infamous Gunfight at the OK Corral, Boothill Graveyard, and the World's Largest Rose Bush. She loved weird historical sites and old west memorabilia. We had a blast hanging out and reading about all the crazy stuff that allegedly happened during the heyday of that town.

My mom was not an impulsive woman by any means, but she was fun and liked to be silly with me. My favorite memories are just of laughing with her until we cried about the dumbest stuff. When we got to Austin, we had an afternoon to hang out before meeting up with her friend, and we walked by a tattoo shop. She didn't have any tattoos, and I think my dad was not a massive fan of them, but he loved her so much that she knew he wouldn't be mad for long. So, we went in, and I got her name and the heart, and she got "M and J" for mine and Jackson's first names inside a heart, also small, on the nape of her neck. She was so excited to tell Jackson. It was the cutest thing. I will always hold that memory so close to me."

"Thank you for sharing that. It's so beautiful, and I can see so much of what you described about your mom in you." I say, rubbing her back in slow circles.

"Thank you. My beautiful mother was a truly amazing person, and I'm honored to have her in my blood." She smiles, melting into me.

She inhales deeply, and for a minute, I think she might decide to stay, but she sits up and places her hands squarely

221

on my shoulders and looks me in the eyes, "Jake, I have had such a wonderful night, but I'm going to go to my room now." She places a gentle kiss on my lips, and it takes every fiber of my restraint not to peel my shirt off her and begin making love to her again. But she stands, picking up her clothes, and walks inside. Leaving me wondering what comes next.

24 Mallory

When I come out of the bathroom, dress on, hair somewhat smoothed, enough to get back to my room with minimal walk of shame vibes, and shoes in hand, I see Jake sitting on the edge of his bed, in his boxer briefs and his shirt still off, looking good enough to eat. His hair is still mussed and sexy, and he's looking at me hopefully. I see the question in his eyes, wondering if I have to leave. I smile and look down at his shirt in my hand. I've folded it and walk to him, handing it over. Instead of taking the shirt, he grabs my wrist and pulls me between his thighs. I feel myself exhale a startled breath, and he holds me by my hips, wrapping his legs around mine.

Pressing his forehead to my stomach and breathing into me, he speaks quietly, "Stay. I don't want this to end." He looks up with his beautiful dark eyes, and for a moment I think I might say yes. I drop my shoes next to him and run my hands through his hair. He tips his head back further to look up into my eyes, and we hold each other's gaze for what feels like minutes but is somehow not long enough. This gesture seems almost more intimate than the sex we had. There is a depth to the closeness that I can't explain, but it feels so good. It feels a lot like my heart might be healing.

I take a few deep breaths, trying to gather my thoughts and rein in my emotions.

"I need to slow this down. My emotions are in high gear, and I can't make any decisions based on what I feel right now. So much has happened this week, and even more in the last 12 hours. I have loved every minute, Jake, but I need to go. You have my number." I say sincerely.

He nods and stands and pulls me into a hug, "Ok. Can I call you? I want to see you again."

I breathe out, the fear of reliving what I've endured in the past and the excitement for what could happen in the future are at war in my heart and mind, but I say "Yes. Call me."

He wraps his fingers in the hair at the nape of my neck and pulls me up to him. His lips brush softly at first, and his other arm reaches around my back, drawing me against his chest, sending a rush of heat through me. The pressure and intensity of his lips are almost more than I can take. It feels like he is sending me a million messages in a straightforward press of the lips, and all of them are how badly he wants me. I press my hands to his chest, knowing that if I don't break the kiss, I won't leave. And I have to go.

"Thank you for a lovely time," I say, looking back as I open the door, and he hands me my shoes.

As the door closes behind me, I hear him call out, "I'm already calling you."

And sure enough, my phone is buzzing with his name on the screen. I answer with a smile, "What, creeper?"

He laughs loudly, "I just wanted to say that I have never had such an amazing time with anyone. You made me believe in just a few short days that my heart isn't completely jaded and dead. I don't just hook up with people. I think there is some weird universal force drawing us together, and it freaks me out. But I'm interested to see where it takes us. I hope you are, too. And if this is too much. Just pretend I never called, and we'll start where you left me at the door. Ok?"

I can't speak.

"Mallory? Are you there?" He says.

"Yes." I breathe. "Jake?"

"Yeah?"

"I'm interested, too," I say and end the call.

As I enter the elevator, I hear a woman's voice call out, "Hold the door, please." I stop at the door and look up to see the beautiful blonde assistant. Barbie? Belinda?

What did Jake say her name was? I briefly acknowledge her and can't help but smile when I see the voicemail notification pop up. This crazy man has already left me a voicemail. The elevator dings and the doors open on my floor. As I step out and head to my room, she calls out, "Hello?" When I turn back, I see she has exited the elevator, and I look down at my shoes, thinking I might have dropped one without noticing.

She smiles sweetly and says, "Sorry to bother you, but did you just come out of Jake Reyes' room?" I'm shocked that she has the nerve to be so invasive, and I say, "Well, not that it's any of your business, but yes."

"I'm his assistant, Bethany." She holds out a hand to shake.

Bethany! That's it!

"You're the lemonade stand girl, right?"

I don't know where this is going, but I don't like her tone. I feel like the way she says it makes me feel like she's reducing me for her own gain. This woman does not feel like a girl's girl.

"I am," I respond tersely. "The owner of Squeeze the Day. Is there something you needed? I'm trying to get to bed."

"Oh, I'm sure." She says, condescendingly looking me up and down. "We ladies need our beauty sleep. Am I right? Well, let me get to the point, from one girl to another, you know, girl code and all. We have to take care of each other. Um, just a word of warning, Mr. Reyes is a bit of a player. I don't know what happened between you, but I can guess, and it's a pattern with him. He isn't serious about anything but his work. I hate to be the bearer of bad news, but this won't end well for you. You will get your heart broken. You'll be one in a long line of sad girls who thought they could be his "one". It's best to get out before that happens. Trust me on this. Okay, sweetie?"

I'm flustered at first, my cheeks heating, and then I feel a sense of clarity and shift into self-preservation mode. "Oh, trust me, love, I have no intention of going any further with him. We had a fun night, and we are moving on. I'm fully aware of what's going on here."

I hate that I said it. I don't believe it at all. I really thought there might be potential for us. But now the seed of doubt I had has been watered, and I can't see any other way but to get out quick.

She places her hand at her chest and breathes a sigh of relief; I'm not sure if it's for her or me.

"Oh, thank goodness. If I can save at least one girl from a broken heart, I've done my job. I do love Jake, and he's a great boss, but boyfriend material he is NOT. He is a heartbreaker, for sure! Ok, girl. Have a good night. I hope everything works out for your little stand." She turns with a smirk.

I can't resist calling out, "Oh, one thing, Brittany." I'm an asshole, I'll admit.

"It's Bethany." She says tersely.

"Oh, right. Of course. This little bit of 'information' doesn't have anything to do with Mr. Reyes shutting you down on no uncertain terms from starting anything romantic with him, does it?" I purse my lips inquisitively.

She hits the elevator button a few times, looking furtively right and left, clearly wishing it would hurry up, "I have no idea what you mean. I work for him, nothing more. I'm trying to help a sister out." She drawls, wiggles her fingers in a wave, and disappears through the open doors.

I sigh, opening the door to my room. As the door closes, I press my back against it, and immediately the tears flow. I'm not sure why I'm crying. Maybe they are for the pain from past hurts, or from the emotion of the day. The fear of possibly losing this potentially amazing man before it even gets started, or just the sheer frustration that this woman dared to come at me like that. I feel in my heart she is just hurting as well, but fuck it, that was just mean. Why did she have to do that? Now I'm really second-guessing this whole Jake situation. He really seemed sincere. Is he that good at fooling women into believing there is a chance of something real, only to drop it? Fuck. Why did I let myself get to this point? Traitorous heart.

I head to the shower and try to cry it out as the hot water runs over my head. When I finally get into bed, I'm exhausted. I'm exhausted from the event, the concert, and then the emotional roller coaster I've already been on after only knowing this guy for a few days. I don't think I'm ready to put my heart out there like this yet. I thought I was. He seemed so different and thoughtful (not to mention the mind-blowing sex), but clearly, I was blinded. I guess I should be thanking Bethany for the ambush. I fall asleep berating myself once again for allowing a man to dupe me into trusting him.

I awake not feeling any more rested than when I went to bed. I tossed and turned, and finally, at 6 am, decided to go ahead and pack up to head home. I thought maybe I'd meet Jake for breakfast, but decided that it would be better to cut my losses and move on. The possibility that our paths may cross with work is always there, but I will cross that bridge if it ever comes to it. I look at my phone through bleary eyes and see a voicemail notification from him, but I can't bring myself to listen to it. It only promises to hurt me even more. Not yet.

I send a quick text to Charley and Whit.

Mal: Hey, ladies. I had a blast this week with you. I'm getting an early start on my way home this morning.

Whitney: Girl. What happened last night? Charley said you left with the hottie from the hotel?

Charley: Um, hello? Are we not going to talk about what happened after we left you and Jake?

Mal: I might ask the same of you. What did you and Sam do? You were looking pretty chummy when you left.

Charley: Oh no, you don't, Miss Thang. No deflection. WHAT HAPPENED?

Mal: Damn. Fine.

Mal:…

Mal:…

Whit: Hey! Focus!

Mal: Ok, sorry. I'm trying to pack up. Um. Well, we came back to the hotel and…

Charley: AND? Did he ravage you? Did he make you the queen of orgasms?

Mal: Oh my god. I'm not doing this. We slept together, and yes, he's got the dick of a god; there were orgasms. But that's it. We are just friends.

Whit: Excuse me? Orgasms multiple? Like, how many and why would you want to be "just friends" with a man with a god-like dick? Not even friends with benefits?

Charley: What happened? I thought you were going to let yourself like him. Did he do something? Try to have a threesome? Speak, girl. Something must have happened.

I'm trying to figure out how to say this without saying it. I don't want to tell the girls, or anyone, about Bethany, not now. I'm too embarrassed that I almost allowed myself to be fooled again by another player. It's too raw.

Mallory: We don't live close enough. He's a workaholic. It's not a good fit.

Charley: Something is off. I don't believe this is really what you think. He was so into you. I've never seen a man so single-minded about a woman he just met. And you-you would never beg a man you don't know to kiss you. Are you sure there isn't something else?

Mallory: Nope. That's it. It's fine. I'm sure there are other fine penis specimens out there.

Whitney: Oh god. I don't even like penises, penii — dicks — and that sounds very medical and sterile. Yuck. Don't say that.

I've got to get out of this conversation.

Mal: Ok. Gotta go. Starting to drive now. Love you, girls! Kiss kiss!

Charley: Ok, friend. Call me when you get home. Drive safely.

It's just 7:30 as I pull onto the road with my latte and my podcast ready for the drive home.

And I still don't listen to the voicemail. I can't bring myself to do it.

I shoot a text to Jackson.

Me: I'm on my way back. The event went great. How's my baby?

Jackson: We're all good here. Wanda is obsessed with Clark and follows her everywhere. If I take her for a walk, she whines until we shut the door because she wants Clark to come. I might have ordered a cat backpack so she can go with us on walks. Hope that's ok.

Me: Oh my gosh. You spoil those two. I can't wait to see you as a dad of a human baby.

Jackson: Haha. That's gonna be a while. Drive safely. See you in a few hours. XO

A video of Wanda and Clark comes through, and they are rolling around wrestling, which is mostly Clark attacking Wanda's tail and Wanda moving out of the way continually.

I've done the right thing by leaving. Jackson needs me. Right?

Season 3: Episode 36 Is He a Commitment-phobe and How to Dirty Talk

Sara: Ok, Blake, you're taking the lead on this one since you're the resident male on this show!

Blake: (Laughing) Oh fuck me. Well, I can definitely say I know about this topic. Even the gays have this issue!!

Sara: Well, I admittedly cannot say this is just a male issue. I'm a bit of a commitment-phobe, but our listener's question is about a guy. Should I read the question?

Blake: Yesss! Read it!

Sara: Ok, here we go! And just as a disclaimer, this is not for children, so unless you want to have an unplanned conversation about sex with your kids, turn it off or get them out of the room!

*Dear Love Biters, I had a lovely week with a new guy. We did have sex once on the last day I saw him, and it was the best sex I've ever had. I later learned from an outside source that he's a serial dater. What's weird is I really felt a connection with him and thought he was different. But I've been badly burned, and now I wonder if my picker is broken or if they're all just this way. Where

have the guys who want to be honest, settled, and monogamous gone? Signed, I'm Done

Blake: Whooooa! That's wild. Let's unpack…

25 Mallory

But I don't hear the podcast. My mind begins to wander to that day. The day I am trying so hard to leave behind.

She was pinned to the wall with one large hand on her left breast and his other hand under her short skirt; it was apparent what he was doing to her. And by the look on her face, she wasn't mad about it. Her jet-black hair was a mess, and his pants were around his ankles. One of her hands was in his hair, and I assume the other, which I couldn't see, was around his cock.

MY boyfriend's penis was in another woman's hand. In my bedroom. Where we slept, made love, and watched reality TV together.

So, that's how my day was going.

But that's not how it started.

It started as one of those magical days. My coffee tasted exactly right. You know, when the creamer-to-coffee ratio is perfect, and every sip is pure bliss, to the point where it's almost mournful when you get to the last drop. I even toyed with making another cup; it was so good, but I didn't because there is no way I could replicate that perfection twice in one day.

When I stepped outside to leave for work, the birds were chirping in their little feeder, and I chirped back, "Hello, little friends." As though I were a coastal Snow White. I could smell the salty scent of sea spray in the air, one of the many things I loved about living near the ocean. The clouds were those cottony-looking puffs that seemed fake, like someone drew them or glued pillow stuffing in the sky.

As I drove along the coast, I saw dolphins. I thought, "Well, lookie there, that must be a sign that today is going to be a great day. An omen of good things to come." I have heard that seeing dolphins meant land in sight or freedom for sailors. I decided to own that on my magical, perfect coffee day.

I listened to my favorite podcast, "Love Bites." The topic of this episode was "Why People Cheat". I talked back to the hosts, assuring them that this wasn't ever going to be me. My man was a rock, and we had spent two years together, and no one had any thoughts of cheating.

At work as a personal trainer, I got two new private clients and a raise from the gym owner for my hourly classes.

So, I guess you could say things were fucking amazing.

When I finished my workday, I decided to surprise Adam with a fancy dinner. I don't love to cook, but I can hold my own in the kitchen. I bought all the ingredients for green enchiladas, one of the best recipes I have, Adam's favorite, and a specialty of my mom's when she was still alive. I bought ingredients for spicy margaritas and churro ice cream for dessert. I bought a bouquet, because well, I can buy myself flowers. Right, ladies? My magical day was about to get even better.

Today was Adam's day off, and he was home working on "honey do" projects around the house. So, I figured he would love a yummy home-cooked meal from scratch. I planned to shower, come out naked, and lure him to have sex. We never had an issue initiating or wanting sex. We had a great sex life, fun and adventurous. Orgasms a-plenty, if you will. I would make dinner; we could take a walk to the beach, then have dessert and watch some trash TV—a perfect end to a perfect day.

I still had the flowers in my hands. They were roses. They were a combination of red and white, mottled. A color I had never seen before, and they made me happy. Well, they used to. That's not to say I get sent into a tailspin if I see mottled roses and begin to throw things and scream. I have a little anxiety, it's true. The rage is gone. Mostly. I've only kicked the neighbor's rose bush once after that.

I set the groceries on the counter. I don't really pay attention to the pile of things on the counter. If I had, I may have noticed a lip gloss that didn't belong to me or the sweatshirt hanging over the barstool by Adam's keychain on the counter. Or I may have seen there were two used wine glasses at 3 p.m. But I didn't notice. I floated right by all of the warning signs, reveling in the joy of my magical day.

And then I heard the rhythmic thumping. My brain attempted to appraise the noise, but reached no conclusion. What could that be, I thought.

"Adam? You there?" I called.

The bedroom door was closed—thump, thump, thump.

As I reached for the handle, I heard the moan. A woman. Moaning coming from the other side of my bedroom door.

She was coming alright.

They didn't hear me at first. I was quiet as a mouse. But then the bitch saw me. He had his hand under her skirt;

his pants were around his ankles. Her top was unbuttoned, and one tit, the one in his hand, was out of her bra. She saw me, and her eyes went wide; she stopped moaning. I think she stopped breathing. Was this a kindness, or did I abruptly end her orgasm? Who the fuck knows? I hope it was the latter. I like to believe I blue balled her so hard.

"Adam." She whispered.

I stood there. Frozen. Silent and in shock. Awe?

"Yeah, baby, say my name." He responded, fully engulfed in what he was doing.

She pointed over his shoulder, "No, look, ADAM," and he turned. I'm not sure what he expected to see, but I can sure as hell tell you it wasn't me.

She dropped his dick. He pulled his hands away and turned, not bothering to put himself away, holding them up to me as though he was going to be under arrest.

"Mal, it's not…" He starts to say, with a clipped tone.

"Do not. Don't even try the 'it's not what you think'. Because it's exactly what I think. I don't care who the fuck you are or where the fuck you came from, but you better get out of my fucking house before I make sure you never orgasm again." I seethe.

She puts her boob back in her bra and side shuffles by me. I want to pull her hair and trip her so badly, but even more, I want her out of my sight. She goes around me, and I don't move out of her way. She whispers, "I'm sorry," as she side shuffles out of the room. I hear her grab her things, and the front door closes.

"How long, you asshole? How fucking long have you been cheating on me?" I say it with a calmness to my voice that even scares me. I could pull off the role of a mafia boss right now. The smooth tones I'm exuding right now are comforting, yet menacing. And it feels good. He looks worried.

He slowly lowers his hands and puts his dick away, zipping up his pants. He doesn't answer at first. "Can I go wash my hands?" he asks.

"No. You can't. Tell me how long?" I ask again, my voice low and controlled.

"Fuck I don't know, Mal. A while." He whimpers. He fucking whimpers.

"You don't KNOW? Well, let's ballpark it. We've been together 2 years. So, the whole time? 6 months? 1 month? You're good at math. I bet you can come up with a fucking number."

"About 8 months, I guess. We met at the hospital when I had my appendix out." He confesses.

"Oh. Cool, cool. So, did your helpful nurse start sucking your cock in the hospital to help the poor baby get better? Was that before or after you told me you wanted to spend the rest of your life making me happy?" I unleash on him. "I'm not sure what category that falls under, but your hand up her skirt and her hand on your dick in MY bedroom isn't making me happy. News flash!"

"Can we talk about this? We need to talk." He begs, rubbing his hands up and down the front of his pants frantically.

"No. We don't. Because the way I see it, if I hadn't caught you, you would still be doing it. So, here's what's going to happen. You are going to get your suitcase. You are going to pack whatever shit you need for the next week and leave. You have 30 minutes. I don't want to see you or hear from you for a week—7 whole days. Don't call, text, drive by, send smoke signals, or carrier pigeons. STAY AWAY! I'll text you when and if you can come back, and we can talk next week. Got it?" I order.

He stands slowly and moves to the closet. I can't bear to watch him. He's behaving like a sullen child, head hung low and arms dangling by his sides. Not once has he said he's sorry or that it was wrong. And that's really all I need to know.

"I didn't hear you. Do you understand what I said?" I call out.

"Yes. I got it." He mumbles.

I go into the bathroom and close the door. I turn on the water and wash my face, moisturize, and brush my teeth. Was that a normal response? How the hell do I know what's normal? I can hear him rustling around and opening drawers. Finally, I hear the zippers on the suitcase.

"Mal..?" I can hear him on the other side of the bathroom door.

"Just go, Adam. Please." I try to keep the waver out of my voice because I will absolutely not let him hear or see me cry, and I don't think he deserves my politeness, but for God's sake, I'm still me, and fuck him if he thinks I'm going to become a complete asshole.

I hear the front door close and his car back out. I lean against the bathroom door and slide to the floor. And I cry.

After he left, I put the groceries away, and I threw the flowers in the trash. I poured a massive glass of wine and called my Aunt Mel. And I cried, again. But I never looked back.

Adam came back a week later, and he told me everything. He had been seeing the nurse for 8 months. Anytime he went out of town for work, she went with him. He apologized for not breaking it off with me first, but never once expressed regret for doing it or hurting me. He told me he had been "Done for months and just couldn't find the right moment."

Yeah, so, fuck love. I won't be participating in that anymore, fuckyouverymuch.

This painful memory confirms that I'm not ready to jump into a relationship again. Especially with someone with so many uncertainties. At least according to Jake's assistant. She would know, right? Maybe I should call him? No. No use dragging out the inevitable. Let it go, Mallory.

26 Mallory

I see the Channel Islands come into view, and I breathe a sigh of relief. I love living in Ventura and cannot imagine being anywhere else long-term. Going to San Diego to visit my girls is always a treat, but I never want to stay. I love my life here and seeing the pier and the waves breaking on the shore, coupled with the small-town vibe; it never gets old. I can't deny my heart is a little sad as I think about what could have started between Jake and me, but I feel excited to tap into all the connections and leads I got for my business this week. I'm ready to really make this happen. I need to focus my energy on my business.

I head to the trailer storage to drop off Amarilla and then decide to make a stop to see Aunt Mel. It's not often I go more than a week without talking to her, but things got so busy, and in all honesty, what I feared would happen if I met someone was happening. Distraction. I'm coming to a more profound realization that I can't get involved with anyone. Mel and Jackson deserve all of me, and being in a relationship with Jake - or anyone for that matter - is not going to achieve that.

Fuck. I really have to stop thinking of Jake.

My phone vibrates with a text.

Jake: Hi. Did you leave already? I would like to catch up with you for coffee or breakfast before you go. Let me know.

I don't want to respond, but I also don't want to keep receiving texts if I don't answer. I don't know what to do. Responding forces me to explain, and I'm not ready to do that. If I ignore it, I can move on as if it never happened. Unfortunately, there is the nagging thought that we could still cross paths in business, and then what?

I pull into Mel's driveway, and she's outside watering her plants. She greets me with the biggest smile, but she looks tired and a little thin.

"Hi Auntie! I missed you! Are you feeling alright?" I say as I pull her in for a hug.

"You were only gone a few days, silly. I'm ok. A little tired, but the meds will do that to me." She says into my shoulder. "You look sad. Are you sad?" Pulling back from the hug and looking me over.

Damn. How did she always read me so easily?

"I'm fine," I say unconvincingly.

"Nope. Don't believe you. What happened?" She retorts, leading me up the steps onto her porch. "Give me a sec, I'll grab drinks."

She comes back a few minutes later with two Diet Cokes and a bag of cheesy curls.

"You know, I doubt if this is on your list of healthy, approved eating items," looking at her choices.

"Don't you worry about that. I'm an old woman. I should be able to eat what I want occasionally. It's a treat. No one wants a glass of water and carrot sticks when they are sad." She says, shuffling to her chair. "Now, sit. Spill it."

And I do. I tell her everything from the first chance meeting to the part where Bethany stomps all over my delusions with the truth.

She looks at me with squinted eyes.

"What? Why are you looking at me like I blew it?" I ask.

"Well, my dear sweet niece, you may have a little bit. But it's probably not too late. I don't understand why you don't just talk to him? Ask him about it. It sounds like you really hit it off, and there is more to unpack with you two. Did he reach out to you after you left?" she asks.

I look at her, not wanting to tell her I haven't listened to the voicemail from last night. "Yes," I say, "He texted this morning because he didn't know I had already left and wanted to get coffee."

"And…?" She asks, clearly reading that I'm not telling her everything.

"Ugghhh. I didn't answer. And, He left a voicemail last night." I admit, cringing.

"What did he say?" Her disappointed tone says everything.

"I haven't listened to it. I couldn't bring myself to after my conversation with Bethany." I say covering my face with my hands.

"Oh my god, Mallory Rose Sweet! Listen to it right now. I mean it. What is holding you back? Yes, you have been through a terrible heartbreak. What Adam did to you was unforgivable, and I know it will still take time to heal from it, but at some point, you have to give yourself a chance. Forgive yourself. You didn't know. He hid it well and made you believe in your relationship. But you have to give someone else a chance, and that can only happen by being honest with yourself and the other person. If you listen to this message and you feel nothing, you still want to move forward without Jake as a possibility, I will support that. But, if you feel the slightest twinge of hope, don't you feel that's worth investigating? I hate to say this, but I'm not going to be here forever, and I hope that you and your brother can find love again. I would love to leave this world knowing that you are cared for the way you want to be and deserve to be." She says with so much love and hope in her eyes. "I love you so much, and I'm so thankful for you constantly being by my side - like, constantly - but you need to see what's out there for you. Your mom would not want you moping around, wondering 'what if?'. Now, would she?" she finishes with a slight roll to her eyes and a wink.

Why did she have to pull the mom card? I sigh.

"I know. I need to move forward. It's just so hard to let myself go. What Bethany said really stuck with me. I figured I could disappear and no one would get hurt. Least of all me."

"Yes, ghosting is always the mature way to navigate a situation you want to avoid. That always turns out well." She snarks.

I pull out my phone, rolling my eyes, and there is another text from Jake.

"Ok, ok. I get your point. You know it's not very nice dragging my dead mother into this."

She smiles. "Well, this feels like a moment for the big guns. Sorry, not sorry."

Jake: Hello? You ok? I'm not sure if you remember me. Jake? Not from State Farm, but last night?

A picture comes through. It's a picture of us at the concert that I think Sam must have snapped. We are standing together with my back against his front and his arms around me. We were dancing, and God, if we don't look so comfortable and perfectly fit together. My heart slightly softens, and my eyes fill with tears. I think maybe I wasn't delusional, and there was something real happening between us.

"Fuck. Fine." I say as I pull up the voicemail and put it on speaker phone.

"Hey Mallory, I know you just left, actually, I still see you leaving, but I wanted to make sure I called you immediately. Are there rules to this stuff? I have no idea. If so, fuck the rules. I had an amazing time today! You might not know this, but I'm pretty sure we're a masterpiece in the making—because that date was *art.*, and I'm no Picasso, but I think we've got something awesome here! Sorry, was that too cheesy? I don't want to scare you away, but I've never felt like this. I'm not kidding. I usually go out on a date and have no thoughts of the next date. I've been called a serial dater, but I think that's just because I've never met anyone who captured me and made me feel so comfortable. Anyway, let me know if you want to get breakfast tomorrow before you head home. Ok. Good night. Oh, this is Jake. Mr. Reyes." I hear him chuckle as the voicemail ends.

We stared at each other. Mel widens her eyes. I don't know what to do. I'm still scared. He seems to be self-aware, but that doesn't guarantee me safety from heartache, and I don't think I can take it. Why does it have to be so hard? I want to move forward and trust again. But Adam has crushed that in me, and although I felt some hope this week, I'm still questioning if I'm ready. Tears are now running down my cheeks, and I'm on the verge of completely falling apart.

"Mel, I have to go. I'll call you later." I grab my keys and head out to my truck. I start the engine, but before I drive away, I open the dating app—64 unread messages. I open the first one. Bleary eyes, I read "Niko, 29 years old, surfer and Entrepreneur". Lord. He probably makes money on TikTok. Whatever. I have to get past this hurt and confusion. When all else fails fuck it out, right? Did someone say that? I think it might be an original. I like it. Maybe I'll make T-shirts, and Niko can sell them on TikTok. Ok, crazy, message him.

So, I do.

Me: Hi. I got your message. Want to hang out?

Niko: …

Niko: Whoa! I thought you were ignoring me. Cool! Yeah. What's your vibe?

Me: I've been busy. My vibe is casual. Dinner?

Niko: Yesss. Love casual. Are you free tonight?

I take a deep breath and slowly blow it out. I'm doing this. Just do it, I coach myself.

Me: Absolutely. How about that restaurant in the marina, Bingo's? 7?

Niko: Done. I look just like my pictures. I promise you'll recognize me.

27 Mallory

He's about 6 feet tall, with blonde curly hair. Loose beachy waves, like the ones girls try to recreate with a curling iron. I like it at first glance, but it is much shorter than it was in the app pictures. I think the longer look was better, but he can't help that now. I hope he didn't go out and get a haircut for this date. That would be unfortunate. Fresh haircuts on curly hair are usually very obvious. Ok, not important.

He's got a golden complexion that looks like a mixture of genetics and plenty of time in the sun. It's a healthy glow and not too weather-beaten. He has a pleasant face and looks happy to be here, which is nice. He doesn't seem concerned if anyone is looking at him, so he's not an attention whore, that I can tell. He's wearing black slacks and a long-sleeved burgundy button-up shirt. It looks good. It's just tight enough to show that he's fit. He's not stuffed into it like he needs me to know he lifts or anything, just fitted enough to indicate he has dress-up clothes and some taste.

I went with a lacy black tank, sheer on the bottom half, with white wide-leg pants, a flowy black blazer, and heeled sandals. I wanted to appear sexy yet not overtly sexual and be comfortable. I wore my hair half up in a gold clip that was my mother's, with curls around my face.

I take a deep breath and decide to let him know I'm here. I raise my hand to wave, and as much as I'd like to tell you it was as graceful as a princess in a parade. I can't. I aggressively lift my whole arm, which I forget is wrapped with my purse strap, and when I go to release myself, my elbow hits my wine glass and sends it spinning across the bar towards the bartender. In a stroke of luck, she looks just at the right time, snatching it out of the air, avoiding any spillage or breaking the glass.

By the time I have untangled myself from my purse strap, righted my glass, and apologized to everyone around me, he has made his way to the bar. I finally stand, trying to act nonchalant.

He smiles a cheeky yet gorgeous smile, "Do you always welcome dates by throwing wine glasses across the bar?"

My face heats, and I laugh, "You saw that? I um, I usually try to be more subtle about my excitement, but it got the best of me. My purse tried to stop me, but I cannot be restrained."

I immediately regret my words, my cheeks heat, and I try to add on, "I don't mean like handcuffed or anything. I just meant, shit. Um, you look great. Thank you for coming."

Why do I always allude to sex stuff to random people I meet? I need to get a therapist to look into that.

Still smiling, he reaches out a hand, "I did, and I hope that the excitement continues." He says, eyebrows raised slightly. He graciously overlooks my awkward comments. "I got us a table. Are you ready to sit?"

I nod. Niko is a lot smoother with conversation than I expected. His texts were very "bruh on the beach" sounding. But I'm feeling more relaxed and a little excited. Maybe this was a great idea after all.

He pulls out my chair for me and gently lays my napkin across my lap. When I look at him incredulously, he puts his hand to his forehead. "I hope that wasn't weird. I was trying to be a gentleman, and then the napkin thing, it's a holdover from a fine dining restaurant I used to work at. We had to place the napkins for the ladies. It's a habit. Kind of cringey, right?"

I chuckle. "No. I liked it. I feel very cared for. Not cringe at all."

He sits and opens the wine list. I look over "So, fine dining? You must know all the good food and wine pairings? Want to order for us?"

He rubs his hands together excitedly, "Oh, yes! I would love to. It just so happens I know the chef here, and he's fantastic, especially with fish. You ok with fish?"

I nod, "Love fish, just no squid or anything that looks like its original form. You know the fish that's looking at you with its one eye." I close one eye and peer over at him, and he cracks up with a loud HA! Like I've surprised him.

"You are funny, Mallory. I'm happy you texted me. Noted. No recognizable life forms on the plate. I'm not really a fan of that either." He agrees.

Our meal is excellent. He was right. The chef is fantastic, and I'm so full. I'm a little worried because having sex on a full stomach is not one of my favorite things. Maybe we can take a walk around the harbor for a bit first. The conversation has flowed easily. We have found we have quite a bit in common. I think a walk would be perfect.

"Would you want to take a walk?" He says signing the credit slip after insisting on paying the full bill.

"Wow. I was thinking the same thing. Yes! That would be great. I need to let my food settle a bit. It was so good, but I am full." I say, patting my belly.

He stands and pulls out my chair, reaching for my hand to help me up. Before I can get stable on my feet, he pulls me into him, pressing me against his chest. He leans into me, his lips at the shell of my ear, and says softly, "I didn't get to say earlier, but you look fantastic. A million times more beautiful than your photos on the app and so sexy. I feel very fortunate that you texted me. Thank you. I feel honored just to be seen with you."

And I wait for the feeling to hit me. I hold still just a moment to let the tingle happen, the excitement for what's to come. But it doesn't. Nothing happens. Nada. And then my asshole brain decides to chime in, "This is where they get ya. They ply you with the lovely food and wine. Pull out your chair and make you feel special, and then BAM! Suddenly, they have their hands up someone else's crotch." Oh. My. God. Shut the fuck up, brain. Not everyone is Adam, ok? We need to get that clear.

I shake my head, and he looks down at me. "I'm sorry, was that too much? I mean, you look great. I went too far. I always go too far." And he pulls away, continuing to hold my hand.

"No, no." I say as we walk out, "It's great. Everything you said was amazing. I'm having a very nice time. I was getting it into my head. I…." I pause.

"A 'very nice time'? I'm not sure that's a glowing review. You what? Is there something else?" He draws his brows together, looking worried.

"Yes, there's more. I don't want to freak you out, though." I pause, gauging his reaction. He looks at me open and expectantly. "But I haven't really dated in over a year. I had a pretty brutal breakup, and I'm just getting my feet wet again. I don't say this to put any pressure on you. I just thought you should know. I tend to write off good things because I have a bit of a negativity bias when it comes to relationships. But you are so great, and we are having such a nice time, I'm trying not to get it in my head."

As we walk, he pulls me close into his side, "Ok, well, no expectations from me. We are just going to take one minute at a time. Sound good?"

I breathe in and out and nod my head, "Sounds good." I like being close to him. But I can't help but notice that he feels different than Jake. Shorter and not as solid.

Fuck. Ok, Brain, take the night off. Please. I want to think with my crotch tonight. You're free to go.

"So, what do you do for work, Niko?" I ask, trying to get my mind off Jake.

"I work in tech. Creating software for businesses and then usually selling the software once it is up and running, and I have trained the company to use it." He lifts a shoulder, indicating that he's not impressed with himself.

"Wow! That's really great. So, nothing on TikTok?" I laugh.

His quizzical look makes me laugh harder.

"I'm sorry. Just from your photos, I thought you might make t-shirts and have a TikTok shop. I know, it's rude and stereotyping."

He laughs. "I had no idea my looks were those of a TikTok shop owner. But, no. I don't currently have any T-shirts on TikTok. Or anywhere for that matter."

"What do you do for work?"

I explained to him how I just spent all my savings to open a traveling bar. He listens intently as I gush about all of the time and attention to detail I have put into it, and when we stop to look out at the boats, he wraps his arm around me and presses a light kiss to my temple. "That's really impressive and sounds so adventurous. I love it."

I still don't really feel that warmth in my body that I'm hoping for, but I don't think I do. I turn towards Niko and lift my mouth to his. There is no urgency; it's just a kiss. He pulls me closer, and our mouths begin to explore. He's very tongue-forward, and I don't hate it, but I'm also just not feeling it. I'm trying, but my brain keeps taking me back to last week. The spark is missing, and I'm not sure where to go from here. I pull back a bit, and he looks down at me.

"Everything ok?" He asks.

I turn and face the water, "Yeah. I'm ok. Can I be super honest?"

He breathes out a slow breath, "Ohhh. Sure, of course. I'm a little nervous, though."

"I'm sorry. "I say, "I just am really trying to put myself out there, and tonight has been really easy and enjoyable. But..." I pause, not really sure how to finish without sounding like a giant bag of dicks.

"Buuuut...?" He questions not giving me any help.

"I'm just not feeling it, and I don't want to lead you on. I was fully ready to go all in on this night, but it's just not fair to either one of us." I confess.

"Ah. I see. Well, thanks for being honest. I was hopeful. Is there someone else? It feels like you have been comparing me all night. Is that accurate?" He says nervously, rubbing the nape of his neck.

"No." I blurt. "Ugh. Yes. I don't know. You don't want to hear this."

"Probably not, but go ahead. We've come this far, and it seems like you need someone to listen without prejudice." He laughs.

I chuckle back, "And that's you? The guy I'm cutting off a date with?"

"Yeah. I guess I'm just a nice guy. Come on." He pulls me toward a nearby bench, and we sit. "Tell Uncle Niko everything." He smiles, and it's just the sweetest thing.

So, I tell him everything, from the minute I heard his voice on the phone, to buying the trailer, to the moment I met Bethany, and everything got messy. I leave out the part about his amazing dick because that would just be rude.

"Well," he begins, running his hand across his jaw, "It sounds to me like you met someone special and instead of trusting your heart and what happened between you, you listened to another woman, who sounds like she's pining for this guy, and you got in the way of that. And, instead of being a grown-up and having a conversation with him about that, fear took over, and you ran, understandably so because someone hurt you, but for fuck's sake – you have to talk to the man."

I'm staring at him, slack-jawed and eyes wide. "Holy shit, you're good."

He smiles, "My first degree was psychology. You're welcome."

"Can we be friends, Niko? I know it sounds cliché, but I need someone like you in my life." I bump him with my shoulder.

He shakes his head, laughing, "Mallory, I would love to be your friend. As long as you promise to help me find love? It's only fair."

I turn and hug him, "Of course. I'll be your wingman anytime. I'm sorry it didn't work out for us."

"Nah. It's all good. I had a great time. And gained a friend. Is it weird that I feel like this was how it was supposed to work out?" He puzzles.

"Seriously, I believe the universe can do whatever the hell it wants these days. I guess I'd better come up with a plan to talk to Jake. Thank you again, Niko. You've really helped me quiet some of the noise in my brain. And I know some woman is going to be so lucky to have you." I squeeze his hand as we walk back to our cars.

We hug goodbye, and he helps me into my car. As the door closes, I breathe deep and let it out slowly. Now what?

28 Jake

Fuck. Why hasn't Mallory responded? I recheck my phone. Nothing from last night's text. Nothing from this morning. I loaded up my car and made a few calls, trying to kill some time. Maybe she got in a quick workout or a walk. I decide to head down to her room; since it was the one right below me, I know exactly where to find her. I quietly knock on the door in case she decided to sleep in, knowing in the pit of my stomach that it's not the case. What could have happened? I'm going to sit at the café and have another cup of coffee. I'll regret this on the drive home, but I cannot leave without seeing her again.

Thirty minutes pass, and people trickle in and out of the café, but not Mallory. Something must have happened, but I cannot figure it out. Everything was so great when she left for her room. I stand to go and smell lavender. My heart races, and I turn to embrace her when I hear, "Hey, boss. Getting a late start?" It's not Mallory. It's Bethany. I feel bad, but I know my face conveys little other than disappointment.

"Oh, uh, yeah. I just grabbed a coffee and was hoping to catch up with a friend before I left. I, um, think they might have already left."

Her eyebrows lift, "Ohhh. A friend? A special friend?" She winks.

Her tone makes me uncomfortable, and that wink makes me shudder a bit, and I can't put my finger on the vibe I'm getting. "She was part of the business event yesterday. The owner of the Squeeze the Day Lemonade trailer?"

"Oh, of course. Lovely girl. I did run into her in the elevator last night, late, and was telling her how impressive her setup was." Her voice is syrupy sweet. "I think she said something about getting an early start this morning."

"Oh. Really? That's so strange." I say deflated, she didn't say that to me. Fuck.

She pushes out her bottom lip and draws me in for an awkward hug, "Oh, I'm so sorry, hon. It looks like she ghosted you. You never know about women these days. So flakey"

I stiffen at her contact and gently, yet firmly, push her back. "Are you sure she didn't say anything else? Did she seem upset or anything when you saw her?" I ask.

Her full southern drawl comes out, and she smiles, "Now, Jake, you know I had some wine and some champagne last night. Do you expect me to keep track of all your conquests in that state?"

I look at her, confused. All my conquests? What the hell is she getting at?

Something in her voice is telling me she's not being sincere. I hear that twinge of jealousy, and I'm sure this woman is up to something, and be sure if I find out she's somehow interfered with Mallory and me, it's not going to be a good day for her.

29 Jake

It's been 6 days—still no response from my way too many texts and voice memos. After the last text, I started to feel stalkerish, so I decided to give it a rest. I can't figure out what happened after she left that would spook her. Maybe she just got it into her head too much. We didn't talk much about her ex, but it seemed there was a lot of fear related to that, and maybe she just wasn't ready. I want to try, but I am afraid I'll scare her even more. My phone dings with a text. Every time it happens, I try not to hope it's her, but I still do.

Sam: Hey, bro. What are you up to this weekend?

Jake: Working. I'm always working. And trying not to think about Mallory.

Sam: Still no response, huh? You really need a break. Let loose a little.

Jake: We just took a break in San Diego. I'm fine. I'll get over it.

Sam: Dude, a large portion of that you were working. Come on. I have a great idea. I'll call you later with the details. Charley wants in, too.

Jake: Ohhh, Charley. What's going on there?

Sam: We are friends. We have a blast together. That's it. I think it's because we come from such different backgrounds. It's just fun.

Jake: What about Maria? You guys seemed cute.

Sam: Cute? Is that a word you use? Well, she is so cute that her fiancé wanted her back. The fiancé that I had no idea existed. So, yeah. That's a no-go.

Jake: I can use cute. I'm not afraid of exploring my feminine side. Anyway, sorry about that. Ok, call me later. I'll be free about 6.

I head into the office and try to keep my head down. I'm not really interested in mingling with my coworkers today. I have a bunch of leads from the event to follow up on and some consultations to prepare for. I love what I do, and I'm thankful for the opportunities. I think maybe I've set myself up to be way busier than I planned. Spending that time with Mallory made me realize that I might be missing something. I had no intentions of finding a relationship, much less love, but now I can't stop thinking about it and thinking about HER. I never imagined having five restaurants and being a consultant for those trying to make it in the business. I honestly imagined my life owning my own restaurant and settling down. I'd meet a sweet girl, and we would have a family. How did I lose sight of this? I got so wrapped up in the progress, and the success happened so fast that I didn't realize I was pushing my true desires to the back. Maybe Sam is right. Perhaps I need to slow down. Take a break. A real break. I think some personal reorganization is in order.

So, I call Sam. "So, what's this plan you have?"

We decided to meet for dinner at Driftwood Laguna. Charley is going to Zoom from San Diego so she can be in on the planning. I wish I could ask her how Mallory is and where she disappeared to, but I won't. She clearly doesn't want any contact, and I have to respect that. I can't help feeling like she owes me some explanation, but it may never come.

Charley is on Zoom on Sam's phone, propped on the table. We have decided to borrow a small RV from a friend and head up the coast to camp. Charley has a week off from school and wants to get out of the city. We haven't been camping in ages, so this seems both appropriate and perfect timing.

Charley: Hey, guys, I can meet up at one of your houses next Friday, March 31. I have to be back by the 5th. Who is renting the RV? I'll send money.

"I actually have access to an RV, no rental required. Where do we want to stay?" I ask.

"I was thinking Malibu and Ventura?" Sam responds without looking up from forking a bite of his salad.

I look up at him, shocked. "What? No. That's not a good idea."

Charley: Oh, shoot. I was going to see if Mallory would want to meet us. Jake, have you two not talked? I assumed you both moved on. She said she was going on a date.

My whole body goes rigid. Is Mallory dating? What the hell? I mean, I guess we didn't make anything official, and she did disappear. I'm so lost. The thought of her with someone else makes my skin crawl, and my blood boil. Fuck, I have to talk to her. Somehow.

"I never heard from her after the night of the concert. Did she not tell you?" I say confused.

Charley: Um, we talked. I just assumed you guys mutually decided not to hang out. Oh god. I don't want to get into this. It's not my place. Fuck. What have I done?

"What do you mean? She totally ghosted me. We didn't mutually decide anything. We had a fucking amazing night. I left a voicemail telling her just that and a bunch of texts with zero response. I thought maybe the voicemail spooked her. I don't know, Charley. I'm lost." I'm frustrated now. The ache of not knowing what happened is new to me. I'm unsure how to navigate this new feeling.

Charley: Ohhhh no. I don't know what was in the voicemail, but I think something else spooked her. I really don't think it's my place to say. I think you are perfect for her, and I would love it if you two hit it off, but you have to work this out. She initially said you guys didn't want to do long distance, but later we pried the truth out of her. The only clue I'm going to give you is that your PA may have run into Mallory in the hallway after she left you and put in her 2 cents on the situation.

"What in the actual fuck? Bethany? What two cents could she possibly have? She doesn't know anything. She works for me; that's it." My voice is getting louder, and I'm seeing red. "I knew that she saw her, but she didn't mention any conversation about me. I knew something was off about what she was telling me. Goddamnit." I smack the table.

"Ooook, there, partner, let's chill a bit." Sam tries to calm me. "The customers are starting to look over here. It's not a good look for the owner to freak out. It sounds like you need to talk to Bethany. And Mallory."

"Ok. Sorry." I say "Yes. You're right. You guys finish the plans. Whatever you decide is fine. Please tell me what you need from me, and I'll be there. I'm going to the office to figure this out. Charley, don't mention to Mallory that we will be up there. I want to get this figured out in my head first and approach her carefully. Let me decide how to handle this. Ok?"

Charley: Ok, pal. Let me know if you change your mind. We'll handle the rest of the planning from here. Do your thing.

As I drive back to the office. I'm seething. What the hell was she doing intervening in my personal life? Had I blurred the lines that she believed something more was happening between us? No! I made it clear I wasn't interested. My anger is bubbling over when I arrive at my office, so I sit in the car taking slow, deep breaths to calm myself and manage to calm down enough to call Bethany and ask her to meet me in 30 minutes in my office.

The conversation went as you would expect. Bethany feigned ignorance at first, and then, when she finally admitted she had lied about what happened, she broke down in tears. I'm not entirely sure what she said to Mallory, but the gist was that she told her I was a player and couldn't be trusted. So, it makes perfect sense that Mallory bolted. With what little I know about her past and her ex hurting her, I imagine she decided to cut her losses and run.

I thought I had handled the situation when I told Bethany I wasn't interested, but my words hurt Bethany. When she saw Mallory leaving my room, she decided to retaliate in the name of "protecting a sister". I learned a lesson the hard way, and I had to fire her immediately. But also, she got me thinking: was she right? I had been working so much that any date I went on was just a momentary distraction. I'm now seeing that the real distraction is my work. I never gave anyone enough time to get to know them. Never once had I led any of these women on or given anyone a reason to believe I was looking for a long-term commitment. I never meant to be perceived as a "player," but to anyone on the outside, of course, that's how it seemed. I'm now seeing that I want to make some changes.

I love what I do, but I don't want it to be who I am. I want so much more for myself. I want someone to be by my side to enjoy life, sway to the music at concerts, "look at the water", and talk about silly things like superpowers and lie around thinking about the future. It seems the universe was trying its best to get me to see this by trying to get Mallory and me together, but I guess I fucked that up.

I text Sam and Charley.

Jake: Don't mention to Mallory that we will be there. I want to tell her.

Sam: Ok, boss.

Charley: Be careful. She spooks easily. She's like a kitten.

Jake: I think I have a great idea. I hope.

30 Mallory

It has been a crazy week. I've had six requests for the Squeeze the Day trailer in the last two days. I am taking her to the Spring Wine Walk downtown next week, which is so fun and exciting. This event is one I've been to many times with friends, and to have a spot front and center in the VIP garden is beyond belief. I'm working two big birthday parties locally and a wedding in Solvang, about 90 minutes up north. I even talked Jackson into helping with that one, so we can stay an extra day to hang out and go wine tasting. We booked a place that takes pets so we can bring Wanda and Clark.

I accompanied Aunt Mel to a couple of doctor appointments because she's terrible at remembering to tell me everything the doctor says. I'm really trying to keep up on her treatments and make sure she eats healthy. Unfortunately, I cannot be with her every minute (I know she's not mad about this), so I can't catch her drinking one too many glasses of Prosecco or eating all the cheesy curls. I know she needs to be allowed to enjoy her time here on earth, I'm just afraid to lose her. It's not fair to her to hover, and I'm trying to maintain a little distance. Thankfully, the lemonade stand is keeping me busy.

Sadly, I still feel like something is missing.

I still can't bring myself to text or call Jake as much as I want to. I got busy, and now it feels awkward that so much time has passed. And if I'm being honest, I don't know what to say. Do I tell him I'm scared of getting hurt? I think he knows this. Do I tell him the story of Adam? I'm not sure I want him to know, yet. I'm embarrassed by what happened, and it's still so painful. I suck at being vulnerable. I've never been good at going deep in my feelings with anyone. And we just met. Sure, we had a fantastic connection and unbelievable sex that, yes, I really want to do that again, but does that mean I have to bare my soul for him? My deepest and darkest thoughts and feelings? I don't do that. Could I, though? I did feel a connection with him, and it seemed like the chance meetings were becoming laughable. I'm just so unsure and confused.

I want to allow myself the joy and excitement of being in a new relationship, especially with a man like him, but I have a hard time believing I deserve it. Do I trust that he's really who he says he is, or do I think that Bethany was right and he's just another player out to use me and be there only when it's convenient? He's a self-proclaimed workaholic and rightly so. He's running an extensive restaurant chain, and who am I to take him from that? And, he's not local. It just doesn't seem to be in the cards for me currently. Maybe never, and I'm making peace with that.

My phone vibrates, and I pull it out of my pocket to see an unknown local number. I don't often answer numbers I don't know, but with Mel's cancer, I answer every call just in case there is an emergency.

"Hello?"

"Is this Mallory Sweet?" a woman's voice asks.

"Yes," I say, already hearing things in the background that sound suspiciously like the hospital.

"This is Community Memorial ER. We have Melanie Robertson here. The paramedics brought her in. She's a little disoriented after the fall, but she's ok. You are her emergency contact. We do need you to come down if you can to help us out with some paperwork and answer a few questions if possible." The woman says.

"The fall? What happened? I mean, of course. I'll be right there." I rush to answer and hang up before she can say anything else.

When I get to the ER, the nurse guides me back to where Mel is in a bed attached to monitors and oxygen. I rush in and hug her tight, beginning to cry. She pulls up the oxygen mask and smiles weakly. "Oh, now, my girl. Everything is ok. I just had a little fainting spell after I got up from my nap. Just stood up a little too fast." She says quietly.

Tears stream down my face. "This is why I can't go anywhere. I can't leave you on your own. You silly goose! I'm going to move in with you. You probably need to eat more. I promise I'll feed you better. No more cheesy curls!" I sob.

She chuckles softly, patting me gently. "Ok, now. Slow down, my sweet, sweet girl. You'll do no such thing. You are taking care of me just fine. No one could ask for a better caregiver. It was just a little dizzy spell. Really! Ask the doctors. Nothing has changed."

The doctor comes in talking quickly, "Ah, you must be the famous niece! I'm Dr. Evans. Nice to meet you. Your aunt took a little spill when she stood too fast after waking from a nap. She's fine. She has a little bruise on her leg from hitting the bed frame and might be a bit sore tomorrow. We need to make sure all her labs are still stable from her last oncology appointment, and then she can go home. She didn't hit her head or anything; thankfully, she was right by the bed and had a soft landing."

Dr. Evans isn't Aunt Mel's regular doctor, so he doesn't know everything about her cancer treatments. So,

I ask to speak to him outside to fill him in and make sure I'm getting the whole story. Aunt Mel scoffs, "You can talk in front of me. It's my life, you know?"

"Thank you for chatting with me, doctor." He smiles.

In my frenzy, I hadn't realized the doctor was very handsome. But it's hard for me to even think about that with everything going on, and every time I try to imagine anything with another man, images of Jake fill my head. "Do you think she's eating enough? Should I move in with her to monitor her more closely?" I ask.

He smiles at me, understanding my concern. "Well, now. I don't think that is a huge concern at this point. If your aunt had been having these episodes regularly, I might be more concerned, but I think it was a one-off, and she needs to slow down. It's hard as we age to feel as though we are the same as we were when we were 18, but our bodies are not. Getting out of bed, or even out of the bathroom, it's important to take time for your blood pressure to normalize. Ok, Ms. Robertson?"

She rolls her eyes, "Getting old is hell, doc. But I hear you. I promise to slow down. Otherwise, my niece is going to move in with me, and I'll never get a great niece or nephew." She winks at him with a sly smile.

"Oh my god, Aunt Mel. I swear. It is my goal to keep you out of the hospital, not to get hitched and birth a baby for you." I grumble.

"Would it be so bad to see an old lady die happy?" she asks, making her face droop, trying to look considerably sicker than she is.

Dr. Evans clears his throat uncomfortably and pats the end of her bed, "Ok, well, I'm going to get your paperwork going so you can go home and rest in your own bed. Please take it easy and be sweet to your niece. She cares about you." He shoots me a very sexy smile. Damn these boys and their pretty teeth. They get me every time! "Let me give you my number in case any questions or concerns come up, you can text or call me anytime."

As he leaves, I look at Mel with my disapproving eyes, and she looks away. "I'm not trying to suffocate you. I want you to be ok and not end up in the ER."

Her voice is penitent. "Ok, sweetie. I'm sorry. I know you are just trying to look out for me. But can I help it if I want to see you happy and thriving? Don't you want any more of that god-like cock? Or, maybe you can use the phone number of that very handsome doctor to get your mind off things? He seemed very interested in you despite what you are wearing right now."

"Oh. My. God. Shhhh. He can probably hear you! Don't even start with that." I whisper yell.

"We are not talking about that right now. We are focusing on getting you home and comfy. And what is wrong with what I'm wearing? I'm comfortable, and it wasn't like I had time to get ready to rescue you from the ER."

I whisper, "And please, do not say 'cock' in my presence anymore. It's weird."

She laughs out loud, throwing her head against the pillow, "Ok, ok. I was repeating what you told me. You started it. You're a bad influence on me."

And just like that, there he is in my head again. His dark hair and eyes. His lips on mine and his hands all over my body. Our hot night together. His sweet words telling me how beautiful I am. Our sweet conversation. Damn. Why can't I get past this? It was one night together. I know I should reach out, if for no other reason than to clear the air. But I haven't heard from him again either. Maybe it's better just left in the past as a good memory? Yes. Move forward. That's what this season of my life is about. I should call the doctor. He's cute, successful, and I could surely use a distraction. But I don't call him.

I text Niko.

ME: Hi friend. I'm thinking of going on a date with a doctor.

Niko: Oh. So, you spoke with Jake?

Me: ...

Niko: Mallory, I know you think the best way through this is around it. But it's not. You have to talk to Jake.

Me: Dammit. Ok fine. I don't know how to make that happen.

Niko: A simple. "Hi, can we talk?"

Me: Can you do it for me?

Niko: No. Now stop texting me. I have work to do. Call me after and let me know how it goes.

Me: Damn. I never knew I needed a friend like you until I had one. Have fun at work!

Niko: DO IT!

I sit staring at my phone for 5 minutes. But I don't text Jake. I can't do it. I'm terrified, so I do the next best thing. Right?

Me: Hello, Dr. Evans. Is it weird to call you that? I don't know your first name. This is Mallory Sweet. I hope you remember me. You treated my aunt in the ER today. I hope this doesn't seem awkward, but I was wondering if you'd be open to meeting for coffee or something?

Dr. Evans: …

Me: Wow, I didn't even think to ask if you were single.

Dr. Evans: Haha. Of course, I remember, as it was less than an hour ago. My first name is Chris, and yes, I'm single. I would love to meet you for coffee. Are you free tomorrow morning?

Mallory: Shut the fuck up. I'm sorry, Chris Evans? Like…Captain America?

Dr. Evans: Yeah. I know. It's ridiculous. If it helps, he was 10 when I was born, so I don't think my parents were trying to steal the name. LOL

Mallory: No, I get it, but how funny. I'm sure that must be fun for you, fielding the questions. Sorry for being predictable. Yes, tomorrow morning will be great. Is 10 am too late? I'm not an early riser.

Dr. Evans: Ok, let's meet at Brewtopia. See you at 10. Thanks for reaching out. I look forward to it.

Mallory: Ok! On the calendar. See you then!

I'm smiling to myself, feeling like I've actually taken a step forward and taken my life and happiness into my own hands. Jake Reyes isn't the only man in the world. Right? I cringe knowing I should follow Niko's instructions. But I don't. I'm too scared.

By dinnertime, we are back at Mel's house, and she is settled on the couch with her cellphone and Netflix. I stopped by a local place called Souper Heroes to get some soup. They have such delicious food, and most of it comes from local gardens and growers. They make their soup in small batches, so you never know what the specials are. They always have the chicken noodle, which is a personal favorite, so I get 2 quarts and some sourdough rolls to go with it. Comfort food is definitely what we all need.

Jackson shows up shortly after us, and we all sit in the living room to eat soup and watch a true crime documentary, Mel's favorite thing to "relax to". My phone vibrates with a text.

My eyes go wide when I open it.

Jake: Hi.

And there's a photo attached. It's a selfie of him standing in front of my house.

"What the fuck?" I stand up and shout to no one in particular.

Jackson and Mel jump. "Jesus! What is it, Mallory? No phones during TV time!" Jackson says with his hand over his chest since I've just startled them both.

"Mallory! I just got out of the hospital. Mercy on an old woman!" She breathes.

"Um. I just got a text from Jake. He's...he's at our house." I stumble over my words.

"Let me see that!" Mel grabs the phone out of my hand, looking at the picture. "Well, I'll be damned. There he is, and that is one beautiful man, Mallory Rose. You'd better get over there and see what he wants before some other smart lady snatches him up." She puts her fingers to the screen to enlarge it, and a strange look comes over her face.

"Are you saying I'm not smart? What? Why are you looking at it like that?" I say, puzzled.

I pick up Clark, who has wandered in from the other room where she was sleeping with Wanda, and is snaking around my ankles. She's very intuitive and can sense when I'm upset. She snuggles into my neck and begins to purr as I pet her. I've never met a cat who comforts people, but Clark is the sweetest. I think it's Wanda's influence.

Mel sounds wistful, "I'm not sure. He looks familiar for some reason. Probably just my old brain playing tricks. Now go. Get over there and see what this is all about." She waggles her eyebrows and shoo's me towards the door.

"Ok. That'll do, Yente." I wave her off. "I'm going. I'll text you guys when I know what's up." I plop Clark in her backpack and head out to my truck.

The last thing I hear her say is to Jackson, "Can you get me that box of pictures from the back closet? The one with your parents' name on it? I need to see something."

Before I head out, I text him back.

Mallory: This is wild. You're crazy. I'm on my way.

Jake: You have no idea.

As I drive, I'm nervous and confused. What is going on, and why is Jake here? How did he know where my house is? Ugh, so many questions.

31 Jake

I've either done the stupidest thing or the most brilliant thing in the world. You hear of grand gestures, and I really have no fucking clue if this qualifies, but I have to try, and God, I hope it works.

After the days we spent together in San Diego, I knew something was missing in my life. And then finding out what Bethany had done, I really had to evaluate what was going on. When Sam told me how she had sabotaged what could have potentially been growing between Mallory and me, it was a kick to the gut and a wake up call all at once.

I was falling fast and had not realized that my heart was diving in faster, but God, do I want this.

I want what my parents have. Their relationship is something out of a storybook, and they have always believed that the fairy tale was possible. I don't know if I can convince Mallory that it's real and I'm genuine. If she has been hurt too badly and can't see her way to trust that my feelings are real, and even with the distance, we can make it work, then this is a fool's errand. But I have to put myself out there. I need her to see that I'm not the man that Bethany described. I will do whatever it takes to convince her that I'm worth a chance. That we are worth a chance.

When we decided to camp in Ventura, I knew I would have to arrange to see Mallory without her knowing I was coming. I felt like there was no way she would say yes on her own. Is that a dick move? Maybe. Probably. But the possibility of her bolting is real based on history, and I need to make sure I at least get to try.

Ten minutes pass, then 15, and I'm starting to get worried. Could Mallory decide not to come back? I know she said she was on her way, but did I scare her away again? I imagine her parked around the corner, staring at me, waiting until I leave. But, just as I'm about to dive into a cesspool of doubt, I see her truck turn the corner and slow down when she sees me. She turns into the driveway and holds up one hand in an awkward wave. I hold up one hand in response.

She parks the truck, and I come up beside it to open her door. My heart is beating a million miles a minute, and I'm sure she can tell. I hold out my hand to help her out of the truck, "Ms. Sweet." I say quietly. I'm momentarily stunned by her. I didn't forget how gorgeous she is, not by a long shot. I am completely dumbstruck by it every time. She is casual and beautiful, and it's how I like her best. She's wearing dark blue cutoff jean shorts and an oversized black t-shirt with a wolf howling at the moon and bright yellow Crocs with green ankle socks. It's confusing why I love it so much. My body has a visceral response. I can feel my skin heat where I touch her hand, and my cock twitches in my pants. I need this woman in every way, but first, I need her to hear me.

She takes off a backpack with a small window on the back, and I hear a "mew". "Who..?"

"This is Clark, my cat. Are you allergic? You can't be allergic." She looks at me quizzically, "Mr. Reyes, what are you doing here? How?.." She trails.

"No, not allergic. I'm…um..it's going to sound weird, but I'm on a camping trip. With Sam and Charley. Sam told me where you live."

"You're with Charley? You are on a camping trip, in MY town with MY best friend? What the hell is going on?" She looks completely stumped.

"Don't be mad at her. Or me. I asked her not to tell you. I wanted to surprise you. I have something to show you and tell you. If you'll let me. I need a few minutes. Can we talk? Inside, maybe?" I plead.

She's hesitant, but I think she sees the desperation in my eyes and decides to humor me and starts walking to the door. "Yeah, ok. Come in," she says.

We walk in, and I immediately fall in love with her house. She has a minimalist vibe, but it still feels very homey, with just the right amount of beach items. There are jars of shells and sea glass. She has wind chimes hanging outside the windows that look like works of art and make soft tinkling sounds in the background. Everything is shades of blue, teal, and green; even one wall in the dining area is a soft turquoise. I feel her in everything I see. A pastel drawing hangs above the mantel. It's an ocean view with a pier and some small hills behind it, which looks strangely familiar, but I can't place it. She sees me looking at it and says, "It's Avila Beach. My mom drew it from a picture from when we were kids."

"Oh yes! Oh my gosh, that's wild. We used to camp there, too. Actually, that's part of what I wanted to show you." I say excitedly. Maybe I'm crazy, but I'm starting to agree with Sam. How are all these things lining up? There are just so many coincidences, and the chance meetings are now feeling like a well-constructed plan from someone behind the scenes.

"Let's start with the beginning, though." We sit on the small sofa, and Clark immediately jumps into my lap and gets comfortable. And I begin, petting the kitten as I speak.

"My parents wanted more kids, but were only ever able to have me, so when I met Sam and his family, it was as though I had received a gift. We aren't related by blood, but we were inseparable, and I needed that. When we went camping, my mom always made sure they planned it so Sam could go with Ivy Jane and us if she wanted to. Those are absolutely the best memories of my life. And they included the trailer. So, when you called and were so excited about the trailer, your enthusiasm won me over, and I was desperate to unload it since I hadn't used it in so long. It was painful to let it go, but I could tell you would love it. It had been sitting unused because I had gotten so wrapped up in my work that I couldn't find the time to fix it up and use it again, which is also why, when you called me and were so excited about buying it, I couldn't refuse. There was something in your voice that made me sell it for way under market. Don't get me wrong, I don't regret it at all."

She's watching me closely and nodding. I haven't freaked her out yet.

"So, when I see you pull up with it in San Diego, all decked out and done so beautifully, it was like the universe sending out another sign, but I couldn't figure out what it was. And then things started getting crazy. We kissed, and my body began to go into overdrive. Not only did I want to know more about you, but I was also so attracted to you that I could barely see straight. Having the night we had was like a dream. Like the most fucking amazing dream that you never want to wake up from. But we did wake up, and God, I'm so sorry about Bethany. I know why she had an idea about who I am, because I gave her that idea. I've been behaving like a buffoon for everyone to see. I was becoming a serial dater, she's not wrong about that, but that's not who I want to be.

I had a bad breakup, too, and was responding like an idiot. I want to be a man who takes care of a family and has a job. I never meant for my work to take over. I know we barely know each other, and it's a lot to ask of you, but please forgive me for my actions that gave her that impression and, in turn, made you run. I don't blame you at all. I don't know how your ex hurt you, and I don't have to know unless you want to tell me. I do need YOU to know, if you'll let me, I'd like to try again to get to know you. I want to make the effort even though we live in different cities.

I'm so into you, and I think weirdly, something has been trying to get us together for a while. I wanted to show you this, just a background of how much this trailer meant to our family. The fact that you bought this trailer and we somehow met after that has to mean something, and hopefully, you'll feel this. And maybe you will see something in me that makes you want to get to know me better, too. She wipes her eyes as I hand her the picture. As she looks down, I tell her that it's me, Sam, and my parents, with the Argosy in the background, shiny and new. Her eyes widen and then squint, looking close to the photo.

"This is your family?" She asks quietly, looking up at me with surprise.

"Yes. That's me, Sam, my mom, and dad with the trailer in the background. We had just gotten it and took it for our first camping trip." I tell her, scooting closer to look at the picture with her.

"But…Jake. How is this happening? I don't understand." She begins to tear up.

I am so confused. "Why are you crying? What do you mean? I just wanted. Oh god. I think I've fucked this up even more." I say, wrapping an arm around her to comfort her.

Clark mews and looks at her, reaching out a paw and resting it on her leg.

"No. Look at this picture, Jake. Really look." She points.

I'm looking at it scanning for clues, and I almost give up, when I see a couple in the background and a young girl standing at a nearby picnic table. The girl looks just a bit younger than me and Sam, and my eyes go wide. Chills run down my legs. I look at her, and tears are streaming down her cheeks.

"Are those…is that..?" I stumble.

She smiles a watery smile and sobs out, "That is my parents and me."

"Holy shit, Mallory. I didn't even see that in the background." I exhale and stand, pulling at my hair. Now I'm freaking out.

"Yeah. For sure. Holy shit." She agrees, wiping tears with the hem of her t-shirt.

"So, if I'm getting this right, this is not the first time circumstances have put us in the same place. We met for the first time 20 years ago. In front of that freaking trailer." I sat in complete shock.

She's nodding, and her phone vibrates with a phone call. "It's my aunt. I need to answer. She's been in the hospital."

"Hello, Mel, are you ok? What's up?" she says. "Oh, ok."

"Jake, this is my Aunt Mel. Aunt Mel, Jake, and I are on speaker."

She puts the phone on the table and puts it on speaker.

"Hi, Jake. Nice to meet you." An older woman's voice comes from the phone

"I'm ok, but I just had a funny feeling when I saw that picture of you, Jake, in front of your house. My memory was niggling at something, and I just couldn't put my finger on it. You looked so familiar. So, Jackson got out the box of your mom's photos and things, and we started to rifle through them. And there are a lot of them, let me tell you. All the way back to when your mom and dad first moved to Ventura..." She babbles on.

"Aunt Mel! Get to the point! What is it?" Mallory urges.

I'm pacing and wondering what the hell is coming next.

"Ok, ok, don't rush an old woman with a story! Geez! Sooo, we finally dug up the photo I was looking for. I'm going to send it over. Here it comes." She says excitedly.

The picture finally comes through, and her phone dings with the notification.

The photo is of Mallory, Jackson, Sam, and me, along with both our sets of parents, standing in front of our trailer. We stare in shock. Mallory and I stand next to each other, linked at the elbows. Sam stands with one hand on his hip and the other pointing to the sky, and our parents have their arms around each other, like old friends. And looking at my dad is almost like looking in a mirror now. No wonder Mel was having a déjà vu moment. Mallory starts to laugh. At least I think she's laughing. It's mixed with sobs and hiccups.

"I *hiccup* knew you *hiccup* when we were kids. How *sob* is this hap *hic* enning?" She tries to speak through her hiccups and sobs.

"Hello? You still there?" Mel calls through the phone.

We forgot she was still on the phone. "Yes, Mel, we are still here. We are in a bit of shock. I'm with Jake. Who, I guess, you know, is the dark-haired boy in your picture who now looks exactly like my dad. Nice to meet you." I say hesitatingly.

"Well, what do you know? I heard about the Reyes family 20 years ago. My sister couldn't say enough nice things about you and your parents. They had so much fun camping that year, and your father was comparing trailers.

I thought for sure you all would be camping besties forever after that, but life got in the way, and I assume you all lost touch. And now look at this: kismet, the universe, or whatever you want to call it, has brought you together at last. What fortune! And, I can't wait to meet you in person. My niece has some pretty nice things to say about you. She seems to think you are a work of art." She gushed back.

My eyes go wide and snap to Mallory, who is now coughing, "Aunt Mel! My god, do you have to say everything that comes into your head? I told you that in confidence!" She chokes out.

I can hear Jackson in the background, "Wait…what did I miss? Jake owns art?"

"You could say that…"Aunt Mel laughs.

Mallory is now calling out to her, "We'll call you back in a bit." And she ends the call before the conversation can go any further.

"Beautiful girl." I say gently, taking her hand. "I don't understand why you are upset. Why are you crying? I guess I somehow thought this would be a cool coincidence, and now it's feeling very heavy. I'm sorry if I've stirred up something painful. Are you okay? What can I do?"

She looks up and takes my other hand. "I'm not sad. I'm overwhelmed. This is a lot of crazy information, and it's been an emotional day. My aunt was rushed to the hospital, which is scary because I still feel the ache of losing my parents. My parents were amazing people who cared for everyone and made people feel loved and included, just like your family did for you with Sam and all of your camping trips. Then you show up on my literal doorstep with photo proof that someone somewhere is determined we give this thing a chance. It's a lot for one day."

"Jake?" She says.

"Yeah? I'm here. What's up?" I ask, holding her close and looking at her concerned.

"I have to ask you something, and I need you to be completely honest." She says.

"Of course. Anything. I'm an open book." I promise.

"Are you a shapeshifter? Are you sure you're really the same person?" She looks at me quizzically. And I laugh. I laugh harder than I ever have because this girl is fantastic. She is witty and beautiful and complicated in the best way, and it's all a little scary, but I cannot imagine being anywhere else. With anyone else. How on earth did I almost let her slip away?

"See what I mean about how this would be the BEST superpower?" She smiles, looking up at me suspiciously.

I pull her close, tipping her chin up, and kiss her. It's a different kind of kiss than we have had. It's a kiss full of longing and lust but threaded with hope and possibility for the future. For our future. She looks at my eyes, heavy with need, and she kisses me back.

"I heard you have some art to show me, Mr. Reyes." She says huskily.

I blow out a breath and laugh, looking at my watch. "Well, Ms. Sweet? Is it? I have a private showing available – as it happens, right now. You have some time?"

Her eyes drop to the front of my shorts, where my very obvious erection is straining. "For that masterpiece? Oh yes, I have time."

32 Jake

There are words to describe beautiful things, but none of them come even close to doing Mallory Rose justice. As she stands in front of me, I don't know where to start. I'm in shock. There were so many days I thought I'd never get this chance again. She is just so gorgeous and real, and I get to have her, at least for now.

"Are you going to kiss me?" She snaps me out of my revelry as we walk towards her bedroom.

I stop and turn her, pulling her into a kiss: an open mouth, tongues tangling, and a breath-heavy kiss. I run my hands up her sides and up her back, grasping behind her neck to pull her closer. She pushes away, and we part briefly, reluctantly, as we enter her bedroom.

"Mallory, I'm going to kiss you so much, so deeply and so passionately, you might have to restrain me to get me to stop."

"Oooo, you are giving me ideas. Would you let me restrain you? Because I have some fuzzy handcuffs I've been wanting to try out. Don't make promises you can keep," she says, eyes wild and excited.

"Wild fucking woman! Get in there." I say, shaking my head. I nudge her into the room and close the door.

Her room is small, and there isn't much space between the door and the bed, so she sits on the edge of the bed. I go to her, spreading her knees apart and kneeling between them. I'm so smitten with this girl, but I'm trying to be cool when all I want is to dive face-first into her.

I look up at her, "I have missed you so much. I've missed your beautiful hair and eyes, inhaling your smell, and touching your skin. I was trying to figure out how I would ever be able to move on without you. I'm so glad I did not have to come up with that pathetic life plan."

She holds me, her palms on either side of my face, and looks into my eyes. "Jake, I'm so sorry I didn't give you a chance to tell your side. It spooked me thinking I was heading into more heartbreak, and I couldn't face that possibility. Everything that happened between us was just too good to be true, and the minute I had an excuse to believe the worst, I took it. I didn't even give you a chance to explain anything. And that was unfair to you. To us. Please forgive me for not trusting you, even when you had given me every reason to believe in you."

I lay my head in her lap and sigh, "You are so fucking amazing. Of course, I forgive you. I know that your past haunts you, and I want you to know that I want to work through that with you, as much as you want me to. Just please don't run. If you have an issue or something feels off, please tell me. I can't fix what I don't know about."

And because I need to touch her as much as possible as soon as possible, I begin to place kisses on her thighs, moving from one side to the other and up towards the warmth between her legs. I slide my hands up under the bottom of her shorts and look at her, questioning if she's ok with this. "I know we just made up, but I would really love to take your clothes off and apologize properly. I actually hear make-up sex is pretty fantastic."

She stands with a wicked smile playing on her plush lips, unbuttoning her shorts and pushing them down with her underwear, and steps out of them. I guide her back into a sitting position and smile, just looking at her and trying to figure out how I am so lucky to have this beautiful woman. I continue my journey, kissing up her other thigh to the apex. I am so fucking lucky. She wraps a hand around the back of my head, pulling my face between her legs, and whispers, "I've heard this story about make-up sex as well, but I've never tried it. And, for the record, I've never been more ok about anything. I've thought about you and missed you so much. Also, I need that magical tongue."

I laugh, feigning shock, with my hand to my chest: "I feel so used." But drag her closer to the edge of the bed.

Lying back, she draws her knees up, and I feast, opening her up to me, licking and sucking like a man just coming out of a terrible starvation diet. I cannot get enough of her. "Mallory, you taste fucking amazing. God, I love this pussy. I have missed this so much." I slide two fingers in, and immediately I feel her pulsing. "Are you close already, baby?"

"My god, Jake. Are you kidding? I've missed your mouth and your fingers so much. You're making me come too fast." She moans, "Come up here."

I stand looking at her. Her hair is mussed and so sexy, her t-shirt scrunched around her waist. Her cheeks are pink, and she's biting her lip, looking at me, wanting more. My wants and needs are easily visible under my jeans. I stand, unzip my jeans, lower them with my boxer briefs, and reach behind my head to pull off my shirt. "I'd like to fuck you in the shower."

She laughs. "Is that because you want me in my soapy, wet glory or because you've been camping and you're stinky and want a proper shower?"

I growl, "Baby, I want your soapy, sexy body so badly as you can see." He grips his rock-hard cock and strokes himself, his eyes smoldering and a devilish smile on my lips. "But you may have noticed the distinct smell of campfire and sweat emanating from my body and hair."

"Ok, yeah, you do kind of stink. I was trying not to let it bother me. But I would love to get that layer of stink off you." She agrees. "Let's get you in for a scrub. I'll go lock the front door."

I walk toward the bathroom with swagger. "I'll go get the water going. Meet me there?"

As the water heats up, I smile, and my excitement is growing. Today is a new day and a beginning for us, and I can't wait to see what the future holds. I'm so fucking grateful that she let me in and wants to try to see where this can go.

"Uh, Jake?" I hear her call with worry in her voice.

"Yeah, babe?" I think I hear her say something else, but can't make out the words, so I stroll out, trying to think of something witty to say about being naked, when I see Mallory crouching behind the couch.

"Oh, fuck man! Put some clothes on!" Sam's bellowing voice calls out.

Charley screams with her hands over her face, "My eyes, my eyes!"

Aunt Mel stands gawking and smiling and says, "Oooohhh, now I see what the fuss is about."

Jackson looks confused. "What the hell? Why did you ask us over when you are naked?"

"Exactly! What the hell? What are you doing here?" I shout, grabbing a throw pillow to cover my junk the best I can.

"Jake! Go get a towel!" Mallory screams, shoving me back toward her bathroom.

"Ok, ok. I'm going."

I head back toward the bedroom and bathroom and decide to take a shower while I'm there and let everyone calm down, including me.

So, after I'm showered and back in my clothes, boner handled, I return to the living room where everyone is sitting, talking quietly.

"Well, so that happened." I joke, and no one laughs. "Ok, guys. Chill out. No one died."

Sam scoffs, "Well, my friend, we're all just a little traumatized. We thought you'd call us to let us know how things went, and when we didn't hear from you, we got a little worried. So, we headed over. We knocked for a while, and then we got really nervous because you weren't answering the door. So, we got the code from Jackson and then shortly after that Jackson and Mel just showed up, too, so here we all are now."

Everyone's eyes shoot toward Jackson.

He puts his hands up in surrender. "Hey, what do I know. I'm just a kid. Aunt Mel told me to give them the code."

Mel looks sheepish. "AND I wanted to bring you this. She plops what appears to be an old, battered journal on the table. Look at it later, but it's a journal you wrote when you were camping. You might find some interesting information in there. But, I'm sorry we barged in," she giggles and looks at Jake's crotch. "Sort of."

"So, no one thought that maybe things went well and perhaps we were celebrating? Especially you, Sam? Nice wing manning."

"I don't know, man. I didn't think you would strip and get after it immediately. You stink. I'm sorry, too." He says apologetically.

Everyone mumbles, "Yeah. Sorry."

"But, if it helps, we're all so happy to see you guys have decided to work things out. Maybe we can head over to the campsite and grill for dinner? Or go out? Fuck I don't know. I'm just feeling awkward now." He cringes, rubbing the back of his neck, avoiding eye contact with everyone.

"Alright," I announce. "Why don't you all head over to the campsite. Mallory and I will follow you shortly after, together. If we could have a few moments to ourselves, that would be great."

Everyone nods and gets up to shuffle out, heading to the cars, leaving.

Mallory is sitting in her big armchair, eyes wide and an amused look on her face. "Sooo, those are our friends and family who might need to learn some boundaries." She states.

I go to her, shaking my head, and drop to my knees in front of her, rubbing my hands up and down her thighs. "The moment has passed, hasn't it?" I ask pouting.

She scooches forward and draws me into her chest. "Yes. But you can be sure you are not sleeping at that campsite tonight. I expect to pick up where we left off after dinner."

I wrap my arms around her, inhaling her lovely scent. "Oh, you can bet on it, Ms. Sweet."

33 Mallory

We sit around the fire at their campsite, listening to the waves break on the shore in the distance after eating a delicious dinner that the boys prepared. Charley made dessert. And by 'made' I mean she brought all of the ingredients for s'mores. We roasted marshmallows and argued over the "correct" way to do it. As we spun our skewers, Jake pulled me to his lap, and we each talked about how the "perfect roast" should look. We remembered having these conversations when we were kids and how mom and dad would help us get them just right. Charley and Aunt Mel liked a light golden brown, slightly melty marshmallow, while I preferred mine completely charred. Jake and Jackson wanted theirs browned, but just slightly before charred, so it slipped right off the skewer. The real kicker was Sam. He didn't cook his marshmallow. At all. Diabolical. I actually really don't love marshmallows now, but in the scheme of a chocolate and graham cracker sandwich, I am on board. But the pure insanity of not heating the marshmallow at all set us all off. We then felt it necessary to find out what other strange and unusual food quirks each one of us has.

Aunt Mel likes peanut butter, banana, and mayonnaise sandwiches. I thought Jake was going to have to excuse himself on that one. He's allergic to bananas and hates mayonnaise, so that combo almost sent him over the edge.

"No. No, Melanie. That's not ok. Please stop. I may throw up." He cringed, looking a little pale.

Aunt Mel laughed until she cried at his reaction. "What? It's lovely, and it really sticks with you. We didn't have a lot of money growing up, and sometimes you had to eat whatever was there to make it through a day." She explains.

Jake nods, "Ok. I'll give you that. I ate a lot of peanut butter and jelly as a kid. But it was mostly because I was SO picky. It's funny that I own restaurants now and have some pretty odd plates and combinations on the menu; a lot of things I never would have touched when I was younger".

I poke him in the chest. "Ok, PB&J is not a weird food. Surely you had something weird you ate."

He shrugs and boops my nose, "Let me finish, miss." He pauses, looking around to make sure everyone is listening. "I like to add… a little sriracha to it - PB& J +S. It gives a nice juxtaposition to the sweetness."

Everyone is silent and staring. Sam speaks first. "Duuuude. I have to say I'm intrigued. I do love a sweet-and-spicy moment. And, you know, we happen to have all the ingredients for that very thing here, now. So, what do you say?"

"Oh my god. We have to try it. I'm so full, but we can fit a bite in. Right? What do you guys say?" I jump up to get the items needed. Everyone groans, but I don't care.

We're doing this. I glance at Jake, and his smile is wide. He's so happy right now, and although I would prefer to have him all to myself, I love this circle of friends and family. I think we both need this. It is healing to my heart to have all the people I love most together.

I lay out all the ingredients for Jake to make his creation, and just as we are about to sit down to eat, we hear a familiar voice. "What up bitches? Partying without me?" We all turn to see Whitney walking up the path to our campsite.

"Whit!" I shout and jump up to run toward her, gathering her in my arms and squeezing her with the biggest hug I can manage. "I didn't know you were going to be here!"

"I didn't either!" she laughs. "But I heard that everyone was here, and I had an event about 45 minutes away. I also heard someone made a grand gesture, and my girl Mallory was in looooove. So, I had to see what all the fuss was about. Well, and FOMO of course."

"Oh my god, I'm so happy you're here. Have you ever put sriracha on a peanut butter and jelly sandwich? Do you want a s'more? I have so much to tell you!" I say, dragging her toward the campsite.

She hands out hugs to everyone, and I see her whispering in Jake's ear when she hugs him. "Hey," I call out. "What's that about? No secrets?"

She pats him on the back. "I just told him that if he hurts you in any way, I will personally remove parts of him that he holds dear. Parts that I've heard you also hold in high esteem. Right, friend?"

Jake cringes and covers his crotch with his hands. "Point taken. I have no intention of doing anything to hurt her or make her sad in any way. Ever."

My eyes well up, and I can't believe what has happened in just a few hours. This man has returned to me and pledged himself to me. I don't want to cry. I hate crying, but here we are.

"Hey, why the tears? I thought you would be happy to hear that?" Jake pulls me close and wraps his arms

331

around me. I feel his body warmth emanating, and it comforts me.

"I AM happy. So happy. It's all happened so fast, and it's just a little overwhelming to think I had plans to go out with that doctor and might have missed out on all of this. My joy is spilling out of my eyes." I laugh.

"I would have never let that happen. If you can't see we are meant to be together, you are not looking closely enough. All of the times we crossed paths in San Diego, meeting as kids, and you know, now that Sam and Charley are friends, that Doctor had zero chance."

I smile into his chest and nod, "You're right. It was only a matter of time. You got in my head and in my heart. And now you're stuck with me. And thanks for reminding me. I still need to text Dr. Evans to cancel."

"I can't imagine being stuck with anyone else. Ever." He holds me closer, kissing the top of my head.

"Ok, ok. Enough mush. Let's get back to that Sriracha PB & J!" Jackson calls.

34 Mallory

2 Years Later

There are 1,000 twinkle lights strung everywhere in the venue, and the planners draped everything in pink, yellow, and blue sheer fabric. Everyone dressed in similar shades, from casual to completely over-the-top formal. The venue is a cool warehouse in downtown Los Angeles, with exposed brick and six large garage doors that open onto an outdoor patio. Food trucks are parked at three of the doors. My lemonade stand, an excellent Mexican food truck that has won tons of awards for its delicious Al Pastor, and a fantastic dessert bar with cotton candy, popcorn, and fried twinkies.

When Ivy Jane asked me to be a part of her album release party, I was in shock. This party is a huge opportunity to promote my business and really get my name out there, and it is such an honor to be there. Her new album, Cotton Candy, is an off-the-chain dance album with a few sweet ballads. Sam was so kind to offer to buy my truck for the drinks. I even made a specialty cotton candy lemonade for the event. She let me invite two people as well, so of course Jackson and Aunt Mel had to come with me.

We expected three hundred people, and it looked like most of them made it by the size of the crowd. I hired some extra servers to keep up with the demand and got to put on a fancy dress and be a guest after the setup. I wore a cotton candy pink mini dress with a very low-cut V in the front and straps that crossed over in the back, and very high heels. I was really hoping to wow Jake since I didn't dress like this very often. What a treat to be in the audience again after that first time I met her and saw her perform in San Diego. Things had been so busy since then with the lemonade stand, keeping Aunt Mel healthy, and managing a long-distance relationship. Her career was really taking off, and it was fun to watch, even from a distance.

Jake was often at my house after cutting back on his work schedule and delegating more responsibilities. His efforts to get back to what he loved about the restaurant business were working. We had plenty of time to get to know each other in every way. We traded stories about our families' camping trips, and he told me he remembered my dad as so fun and generous. He was always making up games and inviting the other kids at the campground to join in. I think that's why initially I didn't remember him because we just always had so many kids joining us.

Things were as serious as they could get with us. I had no idea I could love or be loved so deeply and have been happier and more content than ever. Whatever powers determined to get us together had done a great job, and I admit, I am in love. And I won't lie; I've never had sex like this. He sees me and hears me, and it's so freaking hot. He's so freaking hot, I cannot keep my hands off him most of the time.

Aunt Mel is in remission and doing so well. She finished treatments for now, and we're focusing on healthy eating and living. We occasionally allow champagne and cheese curls. The woman has to enjoy her food. She has recently joined an improv team and does shows every weekend. She is hysterical and, by far, the oldest in the group, but you would never know it. She's so up on the pop culture references and knocks it out of the park. They love her dearly, and I feel like she has an added family to look after her. Jackson is dating again but taking it slow. He wants to be sure not to jump into anything too fast again. He's got a lot of great friends, and we hang out a lot, and he, Jake, and Sam occasionally take hiking and fishing trips together. Since Jake has cut back on his workload, he can do more fun stuff away from the restaurants. I'm hoping he can make Ventura a permanent residence soon. Fingers crossed.

I spot Jackson across the venue, and he's waving for me to come to him with a worried look on his face. Weaving through the crowd, I finally got to him. "I've been texting you! Why aren't you answering?" He rushed. "Oh, sorry", I cringe. "I turned my phone down, and it's loud in here. What's up?" "I'm not sure, but one of the servers said there's something urgent at the stand." He says loudly, leaning towards my ear. I give the thumbs up and head towards the trailer.

Just as I'm almost to the trailer, Ivy Jane takes the microphone and announces she's going to sing a few of her songs from the album. I don't want to miss this. Hurrying to the trailer, I lean in, "What's up, guys?" I smile. Amelia has a mischievous look on her face and hands me a card. It just says "Turn Around". With a confused look, I turn as the beginning notes to "Catch Me if You Can" begin to play. It was the first song we danced to at her concert in San Diego, and that memory comes to mind immediately. When I'm facing the stage, the crowd begins to separate, creating a path. I see Sam standing with Charley and Whitney. What the heck? When did they show up? They wave, smile, and give me big hugs.

"What are you guys doing here? I…What is…going…?" I don't get the words out when I see Jake standing at the end of the open pathway, holding out a hand towards me and beckoning me forward. His parents appear standing behind him. I put a hand to my face because, what in the actual hell? I don't like everyone staring at me. I'm in shock, and I can't feel my legs, but I think a little push from behind, and they start to propel me forward.

As I walk, the path closes behind me, and everyone moves back into a crowd encircling Jake and me. He wraps his arms around me, pulls me in tight, and we slow-dance for a minute. Speaking softly in my ear, he says, "You look so beautiful, baby." Then he steps back, holding one hand, and drops to one knee. I cover my mouth with my other hand and squeeze my eyes shut. He laughs. "Open your eyes, Mallory."

When I open my eyes, he is holding a box with the most beautiful ring I've ever seen. Ivy Jane and her band bring the music low, and he begins to speak.

"Ms. Sweet. The universe saw fit to bring us together many years ago. And then, a couple of years ago, we would not deter her. And I am so thankful for that. You have changed me and drawn out the best in me. I'm so grateful for your love and sweet, compassionate, and fun heart. I love your silliness, and you are the sexiest woman I have ever known. I cannot imagine my life without you. I love you so much. Your brother, Jackson, and Aunt Melanie gave their blessing, so I'm wondering if you would do me the immense honor of becoming my wife? As soon as possible." Everyone laughs and looks expectantly at me.

Tears are streaming down my cheeks as I try to speak.

"I cannot think of one thing I would rather do, Mr. Reyes. I love you, too. Yes! I will marry you!" Everyone breaks into cheers, and Jake stands and takes me into his arms, hands sliding from my waist down to cup my ass.

Ivy Jane and the band break into one of their new dance tracks, and everyone is immediately moving on the dance floor with us, including Jackson and Aunt Mel. Jake presses his lips to mine, and we dance like no one else is there. Our kiss deepens. His tongue finds its way to mine, and the whole world is melting away around us. I love this man so much I can't see straight.

As I look into his eyes, I think about how much I have changed over the last two years. I stopped running and decided to face my fears. Losing my parents took a bigger toll on me than I thought it would. At times in my life when I would love to have them to lean on and can't, coming to terms with that has been more difficult than I expected. I have had to heal from that loss and learn to trust those who care for me most. Knowing that Jake got to meet my parents at least once is comforting, and I know they would be pleased with our relationship and proud of my choices. I pull him tighter as I think of how happy my mom would be right now, and how much she would love him.

Becoming a part of his family has been healing to my soul. His parents have embraced me and treat me as their own daughter.

Somewhere over the din of the music and the crowd, we come back to earth as I hear Sam shout, "Get a room!" We look up and smile, nod at each other, and wave at everyone, and he drags me out of the party.

"But the trailer?" I question.

"Don't worry, my love. Sam has it handled with your team and our friends. They have the keys to your truck and will get it back to the storage center at home. I have a surprise for you. Let's go." He smiles and squeezes my hand.

"So, bossy." I scoff as he propels me forward.

"You haven't seen anything yet, my dear. Now get a move on." He says with a playful smack to my ass.

We get on the road and head towards Ventura, but just before our exit, he takes a different route down the Pacific coast. "Taking the back roads?" I wonder aloud.

"Just be patient, future Mrs. Reyes. The joy is in the journey. Remember?" He responds.

"Awfully presumptuous to think I'm taking your name." I laugh.

"Ah, yes. I'm ever the feminist. It's totally up to you." He agrees. "I could see myself as a Mr. Sweet, or a Mr. Reyes Sweet."

We head along the coast, and as we reach a camping area next to the ocean at Rincon, I see it. An Argosy trailer, from tip to tail, is decorated with twinkle lights and a big sign across the side that says "Congratulations!" "What is this?" I say laughing, "Is it ours?"

He parks the car and comes around to open my door, offering his hand. "No. My parents, Sam, Ivy Jane, Charley, Whitney, Jackson, and Aunt Mel all chipped in to rent it for a couple of days for us. It's all stocked with food and drinks, and we have firewood and even stuff for s'mores. And my parents sent rosé from their stock for you. And you can say no, but I told everyone they could stop by tomorrow evening to barbecue if you were ok with it."

The attention to detail blows me away. The trailer, decorations, and food are the most thoughtful gestures from such a beautiful group of family and friends. Jake's parents even got involved from Northern California, and I couldn't be happier. I feel so safe, loved, and cared for.

"Of course, they can come by. I would love that. But tonight, I'm looking forward to spending the night with you, and perhaps you could bend me over the table in there?" I say, rubbing my hands up his chest and over his shoulders, raising my eyebrows and looking into those gorgeous eyes.

I reach behind him and open the door to the trailer. His eyes darken and go wide, his pupils dilate. "Ms. Sweet, my beautiful girl, I plan to fuck you on every surface. But first, I need to hear that you're mine. I need you to say it." He growls and drives his face into the crook of my neck, biting me.

That rumble takes me back to that first time I heard his voice over the phone, the day that changed everything. He wraps his arms around me and picks me up. Future Mrs. Reyes, I think, smiling, and I wrap my legs around him, dropping my mouth to his neck with kisses, biting him gently. "I'm yours. All yours."

The End.

Mallory's Camping Journal-10 years old

Dear diary,

Camp Day 1

The muumuu parade was so fun, and all the nearby campers participated.

"Oh, Eddie! You look so amazing in purple!" My mother laughed so hard. She had the best laugh, and when she did, everyone else laughed. She is so beautiful and always has so much energy. She takes care of everyone. She is generous and wants everyone to be happy, and she always makes sure they eat.

She never acts like the adults are better than the kids. Everyone loves being around her and coming over to our house. Even my friends say she's so funny and that they like it when she hangs out with us. Everyone wants to spend time with her, and when they do, it's as if time doesn't exist.

She has her hair dyed dark red. I know it's dyed because sometimes I help her dye it. She said when I get a little older, I can dye mine, but that my hair is too beautiful to change right now. She piled it into a bun, and small pieces fell around her face.

She was clapping for him, her bangles clinking like a built-in musical instrument, and she was moving her hips like a hula dancer to the Hawaiian music my dad played for the parade. We all join in clapping for him as he swirls the skirt of my mother's favorite purple muumuu—all of the dads dressed in flowing robes and muumuus.

They parade through the camp as the kids, wives, and moms cheer, and I laughed so hard my belly hurt. I didn't know my mom had packed extras for this exact purpose, but I should have. These camping trips are the times when they really have fun, and I love them so much. I try to burn this memory into my brain. My Aunt Mel always says, "Nothing is ever really lost to us as long as we remember it." And I really want to remember this when I'm older. I want to remember their smiles and silliness forever.

Camp Day 2

On every camping trip, my dad comes up with games and activities that involve the whole camp. Most of the time, we don't know anyone else at the camp. Sometimes, a family that my dad knows from his former Air Force days or from his current job will meet us, but more often, he and my mom make friends with everyone there. And I mean everyone.

My dad is an extreme extrovert (at least that's what my mom says), and she would be ok with just our little family. But she lets him invite everyone because she loves him so much. I have never seen anyone else's mom and dad act as in love as my parents do. They do everything they can together. They kiss in front of anyone and everyone. Sometimes it's embarrassing the way they kiss in public (GROSS!). They don't care one bit who's watching. I'm secretly glad they like each other so much. I'm lucky that both my parents are together.

My best friend Marlene's parents got divorced, and I remember how sad she was. She would come to school with puffy, red eyes from crying. She lived part-time with her mom and the rest of the time with her dad, and while she loved them both, it was tough for her to go back and forth.

Mom told me that the best way to support Marlene was to be kind and listen if she wanted to talk about it, and to never speak badly about either of her parents. She said divorce can happen to anyone and never to take sides when you don't know the whole story. I was always a little nervous to think that even my parents, who seemed so in love, could ever break up. I couldn't imagine any time without them.

But anyway, back to camping, one of my all-time favorite memories is from a camping trip to Mammoth Lakes, back in the days before we had our awesome trailer. This was in our tent era, when sleeping outside meant sleeping on the ground and struggling to find the zipper or your shoes to pee in the middle of the night – we hoped no bugs or animals had snuggled in our boots.

The sun was rising when we were jolted awake by clapping and shouts from the neighboring campsites. At first, we figured someone had gone crazy and was leading an early-morning sing-along. That would be so rude! That's as bad as taking someone else's firewood.

Now, my dad was already up, poking at the campfire, preparing coffee, knowing my mom would expect to hold out her hand and have a piping hot cup placed in it. Mom and we kids were cocooned in our sleeping bags, warm, groggy, and slightly annoyed to wake up like that. But eventually, curiosity won. We unzipped the tent flap just enough to poke our heads out.

And that's when we saw them.

Three bears. Yes, three *actual bears* casually wandering through our campsites like they were on a brunch tour. A big mama bear and her two cubs, sniffing around the coolers and stoves as if they had a reservation.

Naturally, my mom went into full protective mode and forbade my brother Jackson or me from stepping so much as a toe out of the tent. Meanwhile, my dad grabbed a pot and a spoon and ran toward the bears, clanging like an offbeat one-person band. He was trying to look brave, but you could tell he was one "bear side-eye" away from bolting straight into the woods.

The bears didn't seem terribly impressed. They meandered a bit, probably debating whether the bacon was worth the yelling. Eventually, after enough shouting and pot-banging to rival a second-rate parade, they decided to take their breakfast business elsewhere.

Lesson learned: you do *not* mess with a mama bear. And if you're wondering where the phrase "like a mama bear" comes from, it's from *her*. Ok. Sorry so long. I'll have something better tomorrow.

Camp Day 3

S'mores!

Of course, the kid's next favorite activity of today was sitting around the campfire making s'mores. We would all claim to have the best system for roasting the perfect marshmallow and argue over whose has come out exactly right. There would always be the one or two kids who put theirs too close to the fire and end up turning theirs into a charcoal brickette (is that how you spell that?). The other kids would laugh, but everyone still ate them. I actually like the well-done ones and would secretly trade the overcooked ones with the cute dark-haired boy from the camp next door, without anyone knowing. He would happily take my light brown ones.

I love looking at him because he has the most beautiful blue eyes. They remind me of the ocean. I'm not really into noticing people's eyes (that's weird), but his were so different from my dark brown ones I couldn't stop staring at them. I made an effort to stop looking after one of the other kids, who noticed and said I like him out loud so everyone could hear. If he heard it, he didn't act like it.

And that made me feel better. He seems very sure of himself. I like that about him, too.

After everyone had their fill of s'mores, the parents made hot chocolate for the kids and tea for the adults who weren't drinking wine. Mom had one glass of red wine with the dark-haired boy's mom at the end of the night, and that was the only drinking she would do. She said, "I don't want to miss anything. Life is too beautiful to blur the edges."

Camp Day 4

Mom and Dad read a ghost story tonight, but it wasn't that scary. It sounded like a Scooby Doo plot turned into a campfire story. The ending was just silly. Sometimes, on other camping trips, it would be something they wrote, or a supposedly true story from the area. Abraham Lincoln has a ton of ghost stories and sightings that they loved to tell us. One year we camped on Halloween, and they read some Edgar Allen Poe's short stories. We might have been too young for them, but we had a blast. Everyone had costumes, and we had a parade and decorations.

Our camping trips never failed to be the hit of the camp area. One year, they told us about the local legend of Char-man. The story goes that he's possibly a ghost, perhaps a hideous monster or vampire. Char Man is no longer the man he once was. Now horribly charred, legends say he is covered in black, burnt, peeling skin, wearing little more than charred bandages, and supposedly emits a disgusting burnt smell. Haunting some of our local areas. Part of the story involves stopping your car on the local bridge, getting out, and yelling "Help Me! Help Me!"

to which an incensed Char Man will come rampaging out of the forest and attack you.

Some of the bigger kids tried it, but nothing happened. This was the year that the cute dark-haired boy held my hand in the dark. We never told anyone, and I don't think we ever camped together again. He was older, so if he was there, he probably hung out with the big kids after that.

Camp Day 5

We're going home today! I'm so sad.

I don't want to leave. We have had the best time, and all the friends I made are super cool! Our parents are talking to the other families with trailers like ours and might start a club. I think the cute dark-haired boy is part of one of those families. Wouldn't that be cool?! I would like to see him again, but who knows?!

I hope that someday I can give my kids the same awesome memories I had, if I have any (and if they have any, their kids, too)! The traditions that my parents started extend beyond just our families. I imagine the families who were touched by my parents' fun and generous spirit have carried that into their own lives and families. I hope we get to come back here again with all of these friends! I will miss them so much.

Ugh. Summer's over.

Time to start 5th grade.

Acknowledgments

Thank you to my husband for never waving on his encouragement and unending dedication to helping this book come to life.

To Christina: Thank you for listening to me babble about ideas and reading revision after revision. You're a real one. Ride or die.

To Camden & Meeche: Thank you for the inspiration of your friendship over the last 35+ years and your encouragement through this process.

About The Author

Emelle Gill (she/her) lives in sunny Southern California, where she splits her time between keeping airline passengers calm at 30,000 feet and dreaming up swoon-worthy romantic comedies on the ground. A former teacher and CrossFit coach, Emelle is no stranger to juggling chaos, which comes in handy as a mom of three and happily married partner of 30 years.

When she's not matchmaking fictional couples or perfecting the pacing of a perfect meet-cute, you'll find her cultivating her composting worm farm (yes, really), feeding the local bird population, or laughing at her own jokes.

Emelle gravitates toward heartfelt, hilarious stories with sharp dialogue and characters you wish were your best friends. If your manuscript involves awkward first dates, grand romantic gestures, or an unexpected twist involving a goat, she's probably already in love.

www.ingramcontent.com/pod-product-compliance
Lightning Source LLC
Chambersburg PA
CBHW020658110726
47901CB00001B/230